SECRETS AND SCANDALS

Sybil Norcroft Book Four

Carl Douglass

Neurosurgeon Turned Author Writes with Gripping Realism

PO Box 221974 Anchorage, Alaska 99522-1974
books@publicationconsultants.com—www.publicationconsultants.com

ISBN 978-1-59433-512-9
eISBN 978-1-59433-513-6
Library of Congress Catalog Card Number: 2014910364

Manufactured in the United States of America.

Disclaimer

All of the six novellas in the Sybil Series are works of fiction and should not be construed as representing real persons, places, or events. Some names of real persons and places appear but only for the purpose of creating a setting in the real world or as a mention of historical circumstances. None of the real people or the real places were actually involved in the fictional portrayals found in these short books. All of the events described were created from the author's imagination.

Dedication

To my family

Books by Carl Douglass

FICTION

<u>*Last Phoenix*</u> *- A Novel of Betrayal and Revenge, A Story of the CIA's Phoenix Program*

<u>*Saga of a Neurosurgeon Series,*</u> **Six Books**
   -<u>Young Coyote</u> - Book One: Garven Wilsonhulme's Way to Success-No Quarter Asked and None Given
   -<u>Anything Goes</u> - Book Two
   -<u>Heaven and Hell</u> - Book Three: Garven Wilsonhulme Takes on All Comers in the Jungle of Modern Competition
   -<u>Long Climb</u> - Book Four: Young M.D., Garven Wilsonhulme, Engaged in a Social Poker Game of Winner Takes All
   -<u>Academia: The Law of the Jungle</u> - Book Five: Surgeon in Training, Garven Wilsonhulme, Fang-and-Claw Competition for Glory
   -<u>The Vulture and the Phoenix</u> - Book Six: Neurosurgeon, Garven Wilsonhulme, the Final Great Fight

<u>All in Jest</u> - Renowned Neurosurgeon in the Fight of Her Life

<u>Gog and Magog</u>—Yawm al-Qiyamah, Yawm al-Din, The Day of Judgment

<u>Finders Keepers, Losers Weep</u> - A Novel of Innocence Betrayed and the Search for Restitution

<u>Sheep Dog and The Wolf</u> - A Story of Terrorism and Response, and the Sheep Dogs Who Protect

<u>Trojan Horse in the Belly of the Beast,</u> **Three Books**
    <u>Though They Come From the Ends of the Earth</u> - Book One
    <u>Dancing with the Devil</u> - Book Two
    <u>Trojan Horse in the Belly of the Beast</u> - Book Three

NOVELLAS

1st Novella - _<u>The End of the Beginning</u>_

2nd Novella - _<u>Uncharted Country, Uncertain Future</u>_

3rd Novella - _<u>Secrets</u>_

4th Novella - _<u>Secrets and Scandals</u>_

5th Novella - _<u>Decisions</u>_

6th Novella - _<u>Running with the Big Dogs</u>_

NONFICTION

<u>On Evolution</u> **The Origin of Selection, Order, Progression, and Diversity–out of print**

<u>Something About Religion</u>—**out of print**

Chapter One

President's Daily Briefing, Oval Office, The White House, Washington D.C., 0600
Present: POTUS, NSA, DHS, DCIA, DCIA-CT, DDIA, DNI, DDII, DNSA, DFBI, DNCTC, and DUSCYBERCOM
Re: Possible breach

The DNI [Director National Intelligence] presented the president's daily briefing, a departure from the usual practice of having the DCIA bring POTUS [President of the United States, also code named NI One for National Intelligence One] up to date on the most recent intelligence developments. The other departure from the norm was the presence of all of the rest of the directors. Usually the director of the Central Intelligence Agency met with the president alone.

DNI Porter L. Hampshire began his presentation, "I recognize that you have called all of us here for an important reason. If I may, let me briefly give an overview of the occurrences and the interpretation of those occurrences as evaluated by the Office of National Intelligence throughout the country and the world in the last twenty-four hours."

Hampshire was a former police commissioner of New York City and remained an entirely direct and to-the-point communicator now that he was the director of National Intelligence. He told the assembled officers about the apparent murder of a senior al Qaeda operative, Daud al Sharif ibn Saud, in Paris three months ago.

The president interrupted, "Is that the Saudi Arabian prince who used Islamic charities as a front for his wide-spread terrorist activities?"

"Yes, Sir."

"Thanks, I can never keep their names straight. Go on, but leave me the brief on the details."

"The three remaining big French dailies, *Le Monde, Libération* and *France Soir*, came out this morning with headlines indicating that ibn Saud's murder case had been closed. The Sûreté officially concluded that the great Saudi Arabian humanitarian and director of Muslim charities died at the hands of one of his security guards, apparently secretly working for a rival faction."

DNI Hampshire spanned the globe giving the intelligence de jour for everyplace where something was happening or changing—Iran's potential nuclear weapons production; Saudi Arabian conspiracies to nuke Tehran to halt that production and to rid itself of an ever growing threat to Saudi security; yesterday's North Korean ransom demands for the three American religious leaders being held hostage there; the German banks' refusal to bail out the PIGS [Portugal, Italy, Greece, Spain] again; the Supreme Leader of Iran's latest rant against the pigs and monkeys of Little Satan [Israel]; and

Israel's bellicose threat to do a pre-emptive nuclear strike on Iran's nuclear facilities in Bushehr and Natanz.

He concluded, "On a somewhat personal note for all of us, I am sad to report that there is another black star being added to the Wall of Honor at the OHB [Old Headquarters Building, CIA]. This is the latest in a set of four in the past six months. The worse thing is that every one of these agents had an Ultra TS/SCI [Top-Secret, Sensitive Compartmentalized Information, i.e. "above Top Secret"] clearance rating with SSBI [Single Scope Background Investigation]. It is the conclusion of everyone here that there is no coincidence in existence that could explain these murders."

"I agree completely and most soberly," President Willets said. "I fear that we have not heard the last of this. From where I sit, the most serious question is not even necessarily who did this, but how could they know about these super-secret officers?"

"That is it in a nutshell. There is no escaping the conclusion that we have a leak, a mole, if you will," the DNI said."

The expressions on the faces of the powerful leaders of American intelligence would lead a casual observer to conclude that this was a wake.

DCIA Martin Edelweiss broke the silence, "Mr. President, we have to be brutally frank here. I realize that you ordered each of us here because we are the directors of the intelligence agencies most likely to harbor a mole. At worst, one of us may *be* the mole. In this age of hackers and cybertagers, who knows? Nobody is soon going to forget the NSA pipsqueak who leaked massive volumes of secret information and then ended up gaining safe haven in Russia. We need to formulate a plan for investigation of this new mole, and we need to keep it secret. I have been involved in three CIA mole hunts, and I can tell you that there is nothing worse that the secrets and scandals we are going to unearth as we get on with it."

"The National Security Advisor and I have been going over a tentative plan of action for dealing with this. He does not have full clearance to know some of the details of intelligence initiatives; so, his schema is rather broad. There will have to be a more specific directive. I'll read you the outline that we have for now," the president said.

"First, and as an emergency measure, we have to protect our remaining field officers who have an Ultra TS/SCI [Top-Secret, Sensitive Compartmentalized Information, i.e. "above Top Secret"] clearance rating with SSBI [Single Scope Background Investigation]. For my information, how many of them are out there in the cold?"

The DNI answered, "Unless one of the agencies assembled here today is keeping secrets from the ODNI [Office of the Director of National Intelligence], there are only six. Two of them are inactive at the present time. I have already ordered those two to find a safe harbor that no one else knows about and to stay put until they are told otherwise."

"How did you communicate with them, Director Hampshire?" the president asked perceptively.

"Good question, Sir. It goes to the crux of the problem since it is obvious that our communications avenues have been compromised. Let me give you a kind of long answer to your short question, if I may."

President Willets nodded.

"Every one of us here and all of our closest deputies were in office well before these murders took place. Therefore, none of us can be trusted. On an emergency basis, we need to go down a couple of floors in our respective buildings and select a newbie to carry messages personally without using phones, electronics, or written materials—someone who was not here a year ago and does not presently have the clearance that would have allowed him or her to have knowledge of these super-secret agents out there in harm's way.

"Next, to begin to deal with the case in chief—the mole—we all must get to a private polygraph company selected by a consensus of all of us here and have our lies detected. And I mean everyone, including me. Then we have to vet our sub-deputies as thoroughly as can be done and get them to work as detectives."

"We need to bring all of our agents in out of the cold, if it is possible," said DFBI Grant Wallace.

"Some of them are under deep cover, but I think most of them can get away from their situations for a while. We'll have to devise an excuse or two that will not alert our enemies that we are on to them, and above all, we have to avoid spooking the mole," Martin Edelweiss, the DCIA, pointed out.

The president said, "We need a leader of this task force—someone who is above reproach, who is new, who is of proven valor, intelligence, and doggedness to sift through the mountain of information that will be made available. And, ladies and gentlemen, lest any of you plan to keep your own agency's secrets at the expense of this enterprise; drop the idea now. On this effort, we will be united, or I will have the dis-senter's job as soon as I get wind of it."

"Should we include all seventeen agencies in the infor-mation loop or in the investigation, Mr. President?" asked DNI Hampshire.

"Not yet. The NSA and I thought that over. We have no reason to suspect that many of the services have any knowl-edge or access to knowledge about our dead agents or to the four still living and active. After we have gone through your services—if we still haven't gotten to the mole—then we can start looking into air force, army, navy, coast guard, marine corps, national geospatial, national reconnaissance, drug enforcement, and departments of energy and state intelligence services; and then, we can branch out to the private sector if we have to," President Willets said.

"Then, our next order of business should be to find ourselves that leader—one we can all hate or love or fear, but whom we will all respect and obey—a tall order for any man," the DNI suggested to the president.

"I have been considering a name. However, I want each of you to write down three names and what the position the individual is in the government. I'll go over them—be patient with me; it will take a minute—and then offer one for your consideration."

The DFBI passed out 3x5 cards and pencils to everyone. The process took few minutes of thought and a lifetime of soul searching, but the NSA collected the cards and had them in the president's hand in four minutes.

"Good job," the president said recognizing that his chief directors of intelligence had bought into the mission fully.

He flipped quickly through the cards making mental notes. Then he took a moment to write a few down on his own 3x5 card.

"This is interesting. Each of you submitted three names. The total number of separate names to make the short list was eight, indicative of success in this administration's efforts to establish a unified intelligence service. What is most interesting is that one name appeared on all of the cards except two. And that name was the one I had in mind. Apparently great minds…"

"Who?" came a small chorus.

"Because of the extremely sensitive issues at stake here, I am going to keep that name a secret from anyone but myself— 'eyes and ears only'. You guys all seem to like code names so well, let's agree on one. And once agreed, all you need to obtain is an order signed by that code-named leader or by me in order to act and to know that you have full legal authority to do so. I will make it a presidential order, but the name will be redacted until it is prudent and safe to let it become known to you. In all probability, the general public will never know that name. So, give me an idea for a code name."

There was a short intense huddle of discussion among the rest of the men and women in the room.

The DNI answered for the group, "It's Gideon—a reference to the great Hebrew spy and later general."

"Good choice. Gideon, it is."

The room cleared; and when he was alone, President Willets made a call to Sybil Norcroft, a well-known brilliant neurosurgeon, a media news star, a spokesperson and goodwill ambassador for the United States, and a well-established ruthless Company spy and assassin. She was one of the four individuals with the Ultra TS/SCI [Top-Secret, Sensitive Compartmentalized Information, i.e. "above Top Secret"] clearance rating with SSBI [Single Scope Background Investigation] left alive.

Chapter Two

Wolf News Network Building, New York, 0640

Sybil Norcroft, M.D., Ph.D., F.A.C.S. heard the unmistakable ring tone of her ultra-secret encrypted cell phone. The ring caused a spike of adrenaline as it always did. She had been home from her last mission abroad for three months and had most of that time convalescing from a gunshot wound. After her debriefing upon return, she had not heard from the Company.

She answered, "S7A3N0D75#Marburg."

The letters were her initials; the numbers were her birthdate—July 30, 1975, and Marburg was her main claim to fame with the CIA. It was her ultra TS/SCI code. Anyone who had this cell's number had to be one who needed to hear that code.

"Is this a secure line?" came the reply.

"Yes."

"This is NI One," the president said. "How are you, Sybil?"

"Nervous, as of a minute ago."

He laughed.

"You are apparently an early bird. Personally, it is draining to have to get up in the dark and listen to a dry daily report six or even seven days a week. I have some news about that, but I want to talk you in private. There is a small gathering of international journalists being held in the Blue Room. You will fit in well. When it's over we can make a getaway to my office. It is probably inconvenient, but it is important."

"I'll be there, Mr. President."

Oval Office, White House, Washington D. C., 2230

"Sorry I couldn't get to greet you, Sybil," the president said, "but I was afraid it would be conspicuous; so, I waited until now when we can talk candidly and privately."

"No problem, Mr. President. I'm all ears."

"I doubt that you have heard much about the newest secret and scandal in the American intelligence community."

"True."

"At the PDB this morning, I learned that a special agent of the CIA has been murdered. He held a security clearance comparable to yours. Worse, he is the fourth one to be killed in the past six months."

"Can't be a coincidence," she said somberly, "al Qaeda?"

"Neither of us believes in coincidence, Sybil. It was likely al Qaeda or an affiliate or maybe even VEVAK [Iranian Intelligence Service]. But while that is almost a given, what is important is that all of the directors of the American intelligence services are agreed that agents of such deep cover could not have been killed in coincidental incidents. The sad conclusion is that we have a leak, an extremely serious one."

"A mole," Sybil said.

It was not a question.

"Yes. So, I want you to avoid leaving the country for the time being and to keep a lower profile. I am going to have Martin Edelweiss, the DCIA, put a security guard on you and your family around the clock."

Sybil started to protest, but the president cut her off, "You are too valuable to be lost. National security demands your protection. Besides, I have an important job for you—even more secret than anything else you have done before. Incidentally, congratulations for being awarded the Intelligence Cross for your work in getting rid of Daud al Sharif ibn Saud. It was well deserved. I was very glad to hear that your wound was no more serious than it was."

"Thank you, Mr. President."

"This is the job. Although your name was kept out of the discussion, there was little doubt that you fit the requirements and were approved by the directors. They believe—in fact, they are all certain—that there is a mole. They don't know who or where or how. That is where you come in. I want you to head up a completely incommunicado, eyes-only POTUS, top secret task force to find the mole. You are assigned the code identifier of "Gideon." No one will know who is giving the order or receiving the information. But, everyone who needs to know and to obey will do so when you use the word, "Gideon" as if it was coming directly from the commander-in-chief. The NSA, CIA, DCIA-CT, and DUSCYBERCOM are prepared to help you set up the mechanics; but after that, you will have carte blanche to get your own staff. You will have an unlimited funding. Just use your black credit card or set up accounts as you need them to preserve secrecy. I will create a top secret PDD [Presidential Decision Directive] for you. Let's see…it will be PDD-3071. That will cover you for almost anything. I am going very far out on a limb. You will be authorized to use extended persuasion if necessary. We must have the mole, and we must have him or her as quickly as possible."

"I'm pretty much a newbie, President Willets. Surely there is someone more experienced."

"All too true. That is why I need you to do this. You cannot possibly be the mole. The killings started before you came. You have no friends or enemies in any of the intelligence services. No one would ever think that you would head up this blue ribbon commission; you don't have the rank; and no one will ever realize that you were involved. I don't want to turn your head, but you possess every attribute required: courage, relentlessness, ability to think under pressure, the rare combination of common sense and high intelligence enabled creative resourcefulness. You won't hesitate to get the truth, and you won't flinch at having to do the nasty work in the night that allows our fine citizens to rest in their beds feeling safe."

"All right, when do I start?"

"Yesterday would be best, but tomorrow morning will have to do. See Mac Young in special ops at Langley tomorrow morning. He is as loyal as you are. I trust him as much as I do you. I don't think I can really trust anyone else."

"Not even Ed Simonsen?"

Ed had been her trusted partner on several espionage missions during the past year. She had every reason to believe he was reliable.

"Sorry, Sybil, I just don't know him. You can contact me on the special POTUS cell phone any time night or day, 24-7."

"I'll remember that, Mr. President."

"Get some sleep 'Gideon'. You're going to need it."

He walked her to the door of the Oval Office, and they said their good-byes.

Sybil's life became more complicated as a result of accepting the president's appointment. She decided to put off calling Mac Young. Instead, she locked the door to her office at Wolf News and sat at her desk to compose a working priority schedule—first for herself and then for the project itself. First off, she decided, she would have to have three cell phones. She planned to use her long-standing personal i-phone for calls to Charles and Cerisse, to Cerisse's school, to colleagues like Raza Patel, and to the feminist and neurosurgical groups of which she was either a member or a chairperson. That would guarantee an easily traceable telephone record—an alibi of sorts should she need one. She already had a special satellite phone for her usual CIA related business—if that could be considered usual.

Her work as Gideon was different—entirely different. She quietly stepped out into the secretarial area and found a lap top that was not in use. She used it for research and ordered a box of twenty-four Burner Kit phones advertised as the simplest, most anonymous, and most affordable disposable cell phone ever manufactured. The headline on the advertisement read, "Made for people who value security and privacy." She certainly fit that bill. She studied the subject of disposable cellular telephones thoroughly before deciding that it was a safe route to take.

Sybil decided that she had to be the most secret person in the world, and was determined to take every measure she could learn about to insure her secrets and her safety. Each of the phones had a separate 30 day disposable phone number and its own charger. Each of them allowed unlimited talking and text for 30 days, and could be used anywhere in the United States. The phones were designed to provide 16 hours of talking time before recharge and 30 day standby time before recharge. That made the phones perfect for travel.

What mattered most, of course, was the fact they were perfectly anonymous. The NSA, CIA-CT, DNCTC, and USCYBERCOM [United States Cyber Command, which organizes existing cyber resources, synchronizes defense of U.S. military networks, and has the capacity to listen in on every communication directed to and from the military] could not monitor her calls. Even if they came up with a way to listen to her, she would be using a new telephone every few days. For anyone without her resources, the cost of the phones would be daunting—$75 each. However, Sybil had the black credit card. She took a cab to the huge electronics retailer—e-Magic—six blocks up The Avenue of the Americas from the studio. Having pre-paid by the government credit card and verified by her use of a fake identification—address, e-mail, landline telephone—she avoided having to present an ID at the store. The box of burner phones was waiting at the check-out stand just as she had requested.

She took the rest of the morning to secure two safety-deposit boxes in different large banks where she could store the information she gathered. She established identities for half a dozen post office boxes for much the same purpose. Finally, late in the afternoon, she rented two upscale apartments— one in Manhattan, and one in Washington D.C.—where she could store her equipment (but not her incriminating secrets). She had to pay the entire year's rent, insurance, and breakage fees in advance for each of them to be able to secure them on short notice. In every transaction where she had to appear in person, she wore a disguise and presented fake IDs. In every telephone conversation related to her secret world, she used a Mini Gadgets VC300 Professional Portable Voice

Changer she had gotten previously from Ed Simonsen while she was doing her training at The Farm [Camp Peary, the CIA training facility in Virginia]. She informed no one about any of the safety-deposit boxes, telephones, post office boxes, apartments, or burner phones.

The following morning, she went to Best Buy, Costco, and Walmart and bought top of the line computers and printers and arranged for the DCIA to have the Company's cryptology division install different rotating-type encryption software into all three new computers. She personally picked up the computers and installed them in her new apartments. She changed all of her computer IDs, passwords, and websites to totally creative identifiers except for the Wolf News sites which she made even more public and accessible. Thus engaged in her new mission as 'Gideon', she expended two days and had not spent a minute on the actual investigation. She knew it would not be long before the brass in Washington sought an accounting.

Sybil tidied up a few loose ends for her work at Wolf News and fielded some questions from the headmistress, Dr. Stephanie Bradshaw, at her daughter, Cerisse's, school, Georgetown Visitation Preparatory School. By eleven-thirty, she was able to find a Reuben sandwich in the cafeteria, and breathed a sigh of relief, satisfied that she had done all she could in that short time to ensure top secrecy.

Then, she made her first call, "Executive 3-6115," the Langley operator answered in a monotone voice hardly distinguishable from a recorded message.

"This is S7A3N0D75#Marburg," Sybil said giving her code ID for the Company.

She was distorting her voice with her new gadget. She sounded like Donald Duck, but her words were clear.

"How may I help you?"

If the operator was disconcerted to hear Donald Duck talking to her at the premier spy headquarters, she did not let it show in her voice.

"I need to speak to Mac Young now."

"I'm sorry, we cannot verify that the CIA employs anyone by that name."

Before the operator could hang up, Sybil said, "This is an order from Gideon. Verify it now with the DCIA. Do not waste my time."

There was a pause followed by a series of annoying chirps on the line, then the operator returned, "I have Mr. Young on the line, S7A3N0D75#Marburg."

Magic.

"How may I be of service?" the special agent's gruff voice asked.

"Mr. Young, this is Gideon. Have you been expecting my call?"

"Yes. NI One informed me and requested that I drop everything else and provide you with anything you ask. He also told me that only NI One, you—Gideon—and I are to know what I do for you."

"Good, then we need to get to work. I have a list. What NI One may not have told you is that we have unlimited funds but very limited time. I have what amounts to unlimited authority in this matter. If you run into problems use the code name 'Gideon' and refer the person who is balking to the DCIA."

It was somewhat disconcerting to the veteran field special agent to receive orders from someone who talked like Donald Duck. He had experienced stranger things and let it pass without comment.

Sybil's cartoony voice then rattled off a series of orders.

"First off, Mac, go up to the seventh floor as soon as we get off the phone and tell him that Gideon requires you to have a full-fledged Ultra TS/SCI [Top-Secret, Sensitive Compartmentalized Information, i.e. "above Top Secret"] clearance rating with SSBI [Single Scope Background Investigation]. Until then, please trust me and help me get started."

"I'm yours," Mac said.

"Thanks. I need a safe, reasonably permanent office. I think we would do best to rent a large house in someplace like Loudoun County, Virginia with expensive grounds surrounded by trees to serve as our office and interrogation center. We will have to convert two very large rooms into separate insulated interview rooms. The most difficult thing for you to accomplish will be to hire or borrow about thirty polygraph experts and technicians. They need to come from state or local sources or even from the private sector—no federal employees. Once we have a list, we will keep those lie detectors going all day, every day. They will have to be seriously sworn to secrecy, taken blind-folded to the site, and will have to stay there for a year without going home. We will have to provide recreation, booze, food, TVs—all the comforts of home. We will have to pay them enough to buy their silence and cooperation."

"A tall order, Gideon."

"And a necessary one. It is also necessary that this happen on the QT and as soon as it is humanly possible. In addition, you need to get a list of all employees of the FBI, the intelligence services, military command and analysis units—including civilian employees—and the State Department. If you think I have missed anyone who needs to be on the list, let me know. For this month, I can be reached at 703-308-1421. That's a burner phone, don't bother trying to track it."

"I have no intention of violating the secrecy of this mission. I have to tell you, Gideon, it is spooky on the grandest scale I have ever heard of. Somewhere along the way, I am likely to need more; so, I can begin to narrow the field. I will add to your list. I will need a couple of hundred secretary-types, and I suppose they will have to live on site."

"Logistically, we will have to build barracks, I suppose. Just don't be too obvious."

"Again, a tall order. I'm not altogether stupid, Gideon. This is a man-hunt. Do you have any leads?"

"As the CIA desk people always say, 'I can neither confirm nor deny any of your assertions'. However, think of it as a police action, and you are an important cop in the task force. I want you and me to conduct the first few interviews. I will need a very special room; so, my identity cannot be learned or leaked. Fix up a room with a chair, a spotlight at one end pointing at a chair on the other end, and a two way mirror. I will need to enter and leave through a side door without being seen. Paint the inside of the room black. Think you can get us started in a week?"

"Hope for two, Gideon. We will be lucky to make much in the way of progress by then."

"All right, but do your best, Mac, please."

"I always do. Ask NI One. I have a suggestion that I think may help. It involves the private sector. Is that all right?"

"You are coming on board because of your brains and administrative ability mainly; so, I am prepared to listen to anything you have to offer."

"There is a private detective firm in New York that has wide and deep connections to a large assortment of private enterprises, including even some gang connections. The PI firm is perfectly legit, but they do have a very useful network."

"What would they offer?"

"Contacts, greasing the skids, removing obstacles, intelligent advice, off-the-grid, and the latest, best surveillance equipment. Most importantly, the CEO is brilliant and has great insights. They don't advertise, but everybody who works with or against them respects the company and especially the boss. He gets things done and does not believe in failure nor does he accept excuses."

"Sounds like he is just what we're after. Why don't you give me his name, and let me vet him and presumably hire him and his people?"

"His name sounds like some sort of cartoon character or C movie private dick. It's Joseph P.A.M.J. McGee, and his company is called McGee & Associates Investigations. I have his card here in my rolodex, hang on a sec."

Mac gave Sybil his number and address.

"Gideon, that is his personal, private cell phone. Very few people have it; so, tread lightly."

"I will. Call me on the burner cell number to report at least once a day at six-thirty in the morning and if necessary again at nine at night. You can call me anytime there is a problem."

"Aye aye, Sir," Mac said.

Chapter Three

It was one o'clock before Sybil was satisfied that she had learned everything there was to learn about Joseph P.A.M.J. McGee. She had made up her mind to accept him as a third ranking member of her personal task force if he proved to be as effective and forceful as his FBI and CIA dossiers and his website suggest that he was.

She dialed his cell phone and used a Dick Tracy voice as her distortion for him.

"McGee."

"Hello, Mr. McGee. Pardon the theatrics, but it will become apparent why I need to disguise my voice if you will spare me a few minutes to present a business proposition."

"Okay, go ahead."

"I work for the government and currently am head of a commission to find an individual or group within the government who is causing damage to the United States."

"My guess is that you are not after a serial killer per se— more like a mole."

"I am not authorized to tell you much of anything about the problem. If you accept my offer, you will have to have an ultra-Top Secret clearance rating, and then I can tell you everything you need to know."

"I'm still listening."

"I will describe what I need from you and ask you to trust me. The first thing after we finish our conversation is for you to call Mac Young at the OHB in Langley. Give the operator the code name of 'Gideon gave me orders', and that should get you through to him. Once you are vetted, you will get your specific and time-limited ultra TS/SCI code. That will hasten the work considerably."

"Lots of time consuming cloak and dagger, 'Gideon'."

"But necessary."

"All right, I'll tell you this up front. My company and I work for money. We will bill you our usual rate, no more and no less. My rate is $500 an hour, and the clock started ticking as soon as you spoke into my phone. I have a second-in-command who will be paid at the same rate, and any other people who work for me are to receive $300 an hour. If we agree on that, and you come by my office and sign a contract, we accept your job."

"Give me the courtesy of hearing the general gist of what needs to get done. If you agree in principle, we'll proceed. Frankly Mr. McGee, I don't have time to come to your office unless I am certain it will be productive. My identity must remain absolutely top secret, and not even you can ever know it even though we will work fairly closely together."

McGee remained quiet while Sybil laid out her ambitious plans.

She concluded with a question, "So, Mr. McGee does that sound agreeable to you?"

"Yes. If I am to start without having full knowledge and without a contract for the time being, you will need to show good faith. I have a company account. You will transfer $50,000 to that account, and then I will begin."

"I will do an electronic transfer as soon as we get off the line. Instead of meeting you at your office, I want to meet at the Company headquarters. How about five o'clock this afternoon?"

"I am presuming that my account will register the 50K and that you will make the arrangements. Unless I hear otherwise, I will be there."

"Have a nap between now and then. It's going to be an all-nighter."

Immediately after getting off the line with McGee, she called Mac Young again and had him set up the meetings and to get the clearance processes under way. She also had him arrange an interview room where he and McGee could sit behind a two-way mirror. She needed to see them without them seeing her.

Mac gave his usual response, "Aye, aye," [I understand and will comply and then I will report back].

Sybil caught one of the hourly flights from New York to D.C. and arrived at 2:30 in time to pick Cerisse up from school. She had called Charles about having a quiet late lunch at home before she had to go out again. He had a mixed-green salad with fresh grilled salmon strips and bacon ready when Sybil and Cerisse got home. Sybil waited until the meal was done before launching into her prepared rendition of what she was going to be doing for the next several months or even a year or more. First, she asked Cerisse what her day at school had been like.

"A bad boy called me names," she volunteered spontaneously.

Charles glowered, and Sybil said, "Oh, Cerisse, I'm so sorry. Are you okay?"

"I've been called worse, Mama. But I didn't like it. I had to ask Ruthie what the words meant. I cried."

"Oh, sweetie, that's terrible," her father said. "Tell us what the boy said."

"I don't want to, Daddy, it was ugly."

"I'm sure it was. But we are your parents, and we take care of you and protect you. We can't help if we don't know what happened. This is your home, and you are safe here. You can tell us anything."

Cerisse's eyes brimmed with tears.

"Okay, Daddy, but I hate to say what he said."

"Go ahead, dear. We're listening," said Sybil trying to contain her mounting anger.

"He said that I was a midget—a sand-fly—and he called me the "N" word. Ruthie told me I should never say that word out loud because it is so ugly."

Charles and Sybil gave each other looks that mingled anger, sadness, dismay, and determination. They were not surprised, however, having expected and dreaded the day when this would happen. If anything, they were somewhat relieved that it had not been worse. Cerisse was adopted. She had been discovered in the Congo when Sybil was on assignment. The little girl was a pygmy, very small, very vulnerable, and very traumatized. She had been a victim of human trafficking and had been used as a sex-slave. When Sybil found her in her small town in eastern Congo, almost every pygmy in the area had been slaughtered; and their bodies laid out in on a barn floor. Sybil turned over heaven and earth to get her out of there, to the United States, and to have her adopted by her and her generous husband. Cerisse became a loving child who brightened the lives of her previously childless parents. She blossomed in the exclusive girl's school in which she was enrolled even though her earlier preparatory education had been abysmal. Cerisse's report on the racism to which she had been subjected was a clarion call to arms for the angry and powerful parents.

Charles was aware that Sybil had to leave for something to do with her latest mission; so, he decided to take charge.

"Sybil, let me handle this, all right? You have too much on your plate, and I want to settle this once and for all. You have done most of the communications with the head mistress. It's time they got to know me."

Sybil said, "Thanks, Charles. You can hardly imagine what a burden you will lift off my shoulders. Both emotionally and time-wise, I will be swamped for a while. So, Cerisse, you were very brave today. Daddy will take care of it. He is big and strong and smart. Now, I have to tell you something about my day."

She gave a thoroughly watered down version of her upcoming project. Cerisse accepted what her mother had to say at face value even though it was part minimization and part lies. Charles was aware of Sybil's work away from her position as the senior medical consultant at Wolf News. He nodded from time to time to let Sybil know that he was reading between the lines.

Chapter Four

Sybil arrived early—three-forty-five—at the OHB; so, she could have a short meeting with the DUSCYBERCOM and the chief cyber technologist of the CIA. Martin Edelweiss, the DCIA, had arranged the short meeting at the behest of the president; and, on his own, arranged for the chief of DARPA [Defense Advanced Research Projects Agency], Col. Avery Holmes, and the commander of the SSG-CNO [Strategic Studies Group for the Chief of Naval Operations], Col. Avery Holmes to attend the meeting. The purpose was to enlist the services of the premier defensive cyber experts in the project. The two men were used to secrets and scandals and acquiesced good-naturedly to being unable to see Sybil or to hear her natural voice as they talked to her.

DARPA is a creative cyber technology military agency known for its "interesting"—here read eccentric and even bizarre—solutions for problems of the Ethernet. Col. Holmes's favorite descriptor for his organization was, "We are the folks who brought you the internet."

Capt. Raylan and Col. Holmes were also agreeable to work hand-in-glove with the odd-voiced leader they could not see and were ready to start that night to put into motion electronic surveillance on every one in or employed by the United States Department of Defense, including the military, civilian contractors, and university people. They agreed to two dozen key words to identify in communications and to apply DARPA's unique software for voice identification to determine to whom and from whom calls were being made—including al Qaeda operatives. They suggested that they be allowed to have the full cooperation of the NSA in order to have access to the NSA's incredible resources. The two senior officers were well aware of the need for secrecy.

Captain Raylan explained the attitude of the two services, and offered an off-hand comment that they recognized that a mole hunt was in progress. They wanted to be aboard.

"We civilized people have built our lives around our wired and wireless networks controlled by computers," he said, "The question is, are we ready to work together for real to defend them and the people who man them in all honesty? There is a small army of dedicated individuals who work in counter-terrorism to protect and to defend our people and the Constitution. That entire group should be included. Homeland Security has a National Cyber Security Division [NCSD] which operates what is called the Control System Security Program [CSSP]. The government has established a program run by Homeland Security which has a computer emergency response team—Industrial Control Systems Cyber Emergency Response Team [ICS-CERT]. They need to be on board fully. The FBI currently leads the national effort to investigate high-tech crimes, including cyber-based terrorism, espionage, computer intrusions, and major cyber fraud. Their assets include the National Cyber Investigative Joint Task Force, ready to roll Cyber Task Forces, InfraGard for protecting infrastructure, the National Cyber-Forensics & Training Alliance, the Strategic Alliance Cyber Crime Working Group, and Cyber Action Teams. Each of those FBI groups should be represented, as well as be key enforcers in the field. And there is the DOJ Computer Crime & Intellectual Property Section. The DIA works closely with them. We can find a mole or a traitor—the same thing in our estimation—and we can do so on the QT."

"I'll take it under advisement," Sybil said in her unnatural exaggerated Humphrey Bogart voice. "I will get back to you."

At five, a secretary from the first floor led Sybil to the special interview room on the seventh floor with a high quality two-way glass mirror. The inside of the room was very brightly lit and contained two metal chairs equipped with microphones. The mirror itself was partially reflective and partially transparent. The brightly lit inside of the room and darkened area where Sybil was ensconced alone in the dark allowed those in the room to see only their own reflection, but Sybil to view the room's occupants. Sound was only transmittable one direction as well.

Mac Young led Joseph P.A.M.J. McGee into the brightly lit interview room. They sat in the two chairs provided.

Sybil's voice—distorted to sound something like a cartoon chipmunk—began the interview, "Thank you for coming and for being prompt. I will reward you for that by making the meeting as brief as possible. The purpose is for you to receive the information necessary for you to proceed if you choose to do so. I have been appointed to be the chairperson of this committee and have been charged to find a highly suspected mole in the government or military. We have a firm basis for our opinion that there is a mole—in fact a murderous mole—who is a traitor to our country. We must identify, apprehend, and extract information from him or her. We have to know how many others are involved and how widely our top-secret information has been disseminated. Now that you are aware on a formal basis, I have the first question? Are you willing to proceed and to put yourselves under the privileges and requirements of the ultra-top secret clearance designation?"

Both men answered in the affirmative.

"Next, is there any reason that you should be considered to have a conflict with becoming a part of this secret enterprise? That is do you have financial conflicts because of governmental contacts or conflicts? Are you, yourself, a sympathizer or enabler of international terrorist groups? Are you physically or emotionally unable to embark on such a venture—once in, there is no turning back; and you will never be able to talk or to write about it?"

Neither man had a problem.

"Now, since you will be in what amounts to a partnership with Mac, here, Mr. McGee, would you please tell us something about yourself?

McGee was used to being involved in serious business and government issues, in dealing with heavy workloads, and contending with prima donnas at all levels. His success rate was impressive, and he was very well thought of by both his clients and even his opponents. His response had been given dozens of times before and was well practiced.

"My name is Joseph Patrick Aloysius Michael John McGee. Really. That moniker was a gift from my sainted mother—

rest her soul—who was more Irish than the Fenians and more Catholic than the pope. She was very young when I came along, and could not make up her mind what to call her first born; so, she used all the names from some Irish ditty. Sometimes, she even called me all of them when she was mad at me; but mostly she called me Joseph Patrick. Having such a peculiar name guaranteed that I would grow up tough—something on the order of being named "Sue" like the Johnny Cash song. I learned to fight in the first grade and earned my crooked nose and the right to be known only as McGee to everyone but my mother thereafter.

"I am a private investigator who came by his profession in an unlikely way. Most PIs were former cops who either became unfit for further NYPD service or retired with a nice letter, a nice plaque, and a meager pension and chose being a PI over being a security guard. I, on the other hand, knew what I wanted to be from my mid-teens. I got a degree in criminology at CUNY, graduating with honors after three years and a law degree from Columbia. My first job was as a CSI for NYPD. That lasted three years, and I quit because the pay was too low and the promotions too slow. I then worked as a criminalist for the FBI specializing in ballistics and then banking fraud for a total of five years. I quit because I could no longer stomach the bureaucracy. PI work is not all that lucrative for most people, probably because they are just not suited for high-end work. My firm—McGee & Associates—does its share of nasty divorce dirt digging and embezzlement work, but our real money comes from surveillance in corporate espionage cases, forensic accountancy, and in-depth investigations for the defense in high-profile criminal cases—usually murders.

"My office is in mid-town Manhattan, is clean and presentable with chrome and glass fixtures and no hand-painted signs by the proprietor—another set of differences between me and the lower class of PIs whom the real cops refer to as "bottom feeders." We don't advertise on TV or on billboards. My clients are largely rich, have serious issues with opponents; or, in criminal cases, they have vices to hide and important secrets to keep. Our policy is to provide the truth, and the clients who pay the bills are informed up front that we will not lie for them in or out of court, and we will give them all of what we discover and let them be the judge of how to use the information. We don't take bribes; anyone who did such a thing would be kicking rocks down the road half a minute after I learned that he or she did. Sometimes our clients balk at such pristine morality, but it has paid off over the two decades we have been in business.

"I have two partners: Caitlin O'Brian, who has been with me for six months. Her former occupation was as one of New York's finest, a homicide detective in the Central Investigation and Resource Division, Homicide Analysis Unit, who ran afoul of her precinct captain. It seems that there was a disagreement about who had the right to do what, with which, and to whom; and she decked him. To avoid unpleasantness of separation with its attendant negative publicity, Catlin accepted a full pension and a nice letter of recommendation. She is a tough black Irish girl from the Bronx who had four brothers—a condition that lent itself to an education in fighting. After finishing the academy and doing her rookie year, she obtained an associate degree in criminology specializing in bank fraud and hand-writing analysis. That proved to be boring; so, the feisty colleen moved to the homicide division of mid-town Manhattan where I first met her.

"My other partner is Ivory White, an unlikely name for the blackest man I ever met. He has something of a murky past about which I know everything, and no one else knows anything. He is—in the vernacular—the muscle of the organization. He is tall, athletic, bald, arrogant, and mean if needs be—and that is often the case in his line of work, perhaps best known by its euphemism—"special investigations." He does all of our personal security for high profile clients. For all of his martial arts and other physical skills sets, Ivory is extremely intelligent. He is a remarkable linguist who speaks six of the most useful languages of the 800 used by the citizens of the most densely populated city in the country if not the world. I will want them aboard. While they don't have to know everything, they are too smart to function in the dark. If they are treated like outsiders, they will rebel. You will have to cut them some slack if you hire me, otherwise, no deal."

Sybil said, "You're hired. Report to Mac and get started tomorrow, all right?"

"Fine with me," both men answered.

"Okay, Mac, take McGee in hand and get him the ultra-top secret clearance he needs. He needs it today. You can tell that to anyone who objects or complains, that the orders come from Gideon and ultimately from NI One."

The rest of the people being interviewed that afternoon were the directors and deputy directors of the principle intelligence services. Sybil had no illusions that her interview would spark a sudden and dramatic confession. She wanted to get a feel for the attitudes and the potential for cooperation from each of the powerful spymasters.

She could not be seen, and the voice she projected was so altered by her portable voice changing device that it came across as that of Darth Vader, which Sybil considered to be appropriate to the moment. The gist of each of the interviews was brief and almost exactly the same:

Sybil:	Person being interviewed:
Good afternoon Mr. Director.	—Good afternoon.
I know you are very busy and are no doubt annoyed by this intrusion which may seem trivial. Let me assure it is not.	—I hardly consider it trivial since I was ordered here by the President of the United States.
Indeed. Then we will proceed with my questions. I only have a few.	—That will be unusual and welcome.
Are you agent of any foreign power, including a terrorist group for personal gain or for any political, religious, or philosophical reason?	—No.
Have you transmitted any documents, electronic data, telephonic messages, or verbal communications to any enemy of the United States or to any individual or organization for any reason, including for personal gain?	—No.

Have you ever been a member of, a sympathizer of, or an employee of any such organization?	—No.
Are you aware of anyone in your command or under your direction, military, civilian, or from any branch of government who has or is now transmitting such information?	—No.
Do you hold a personal or professional grudge against the United States government, military, or civilian departments or individuals in positions of authority?	—No.
Will you submit to a polygraph test now?	—Pause…Yes, I guess I will if I have to.

The uniformity of the questions and answers would have suggested to anyone who could only read the written transcripts that the exercise had been a failure and would continue to fail even if thousands of individuals were similarly interviewed. However, Sybil honed her skills during the questioning. She became more facile with understanding facial and body language and tones and intonations of their voices. She noted, for example, that the DFBI had a tremor which could possibly be interpreted as coming from nervousness. But to Sybil's trained eyes, the tremor was the typical pill-rolling tremor of Parkinson's disease. The DDII [Deputy Director of National Intelligence for Intelligence

Integration] and DNSA both chewed the inside of their lips before answering several of the more pointed questions. To Sybil's eye—which was rapidly becoming better educated— that was suggestive of an intentional infliction of a little pain to obscure the results of a polygraph, and they were following a pattern used before to create a deception during polygraph tests which they knew were coming that afternoon. She made notes on her observations and red check marks by each man's name.

Chapter Five

Two days later the working team was complete, and a schedule of meetings and an agenda was hashed out. Mac was a paragon of efficiency. A site was arranged in Loudoun County, and overpaid and under-informed contractors and subcontractors were already on site. The construction of a serious fence and the installation of security measures were under way. Until that work was complete, busloads of ranking leaders were brought to the OHB to be interviewed in the special seventh floor room. Mac, McGee, and Sybil took turns and reported to each other what they had learned about technique and about the tidbits of information they were gathering.

The CNO [Chief of Naval Operations] told McGee that he had been concerned about the activities of a senior agent in the NCIS [Naval Criminal Investigative Service] and had had his staffers place a tracer on the man's communications. He was not yet to the point that he wanted to have physical surveillance put on the man. Besides, the NCIS was the service that did that sort of thing. He would have to find another watcher.

Mac said, "This is just the kind of thing McGee is good at. How about you doing the physical surveillance? You can get any uniforms and credentials you need from us or from the DDDIA—they call him '3-D'. I'll get the electronic scrutiny underway. I think us spooks should take over from the navy to avoid making the NCIS guy suspicious."

"Agreed," said Sybil. "Are you okay with that, McGee?"

"I'm on it. I'll get the particulars from your notes and start to work on the guy."

The CNO was informed and wrote an order to cease and desist from following the electronic transmissions of Special Agent Myron Jacobsen, who worked in the NCIS Headquarters located in the Russell-Knox Building aboard Marine Corps Base Quantico, Virginia. The HQ office supervises all of the Washington D.C. field offices.

McGee decided to start low and go slow in his approach to the investigation of Special NCIS Agent Jacobsen. He put his partner, Ivory White, in charge of physical surveillance of the NCIS agent, and White used the services fifteen other African-American watchers—men and women whom he trusted. Most of them were his homies. Most of them were members of the same Crip set he joined during his childhood and youth in Brownsville, Brooklyn. He had groomed a group of reasonably presentable gang members who were willing to forego wearing the color blue and facial tattoos that made them stand out and therefore be poor agents of surveillance. Although he insisted that he was no longer a certified gang member, his homies still called him, "Cuzz."

Two of Ivory's agents were enlisted navy petty officers. McGee arranged for them to be assigned to security guard positions in the Russell-Knox Building on Quantico with liberal and flexible working hours and place assignments. That career pathway was facilitated by the use of the code name 'Gideon'. Eight others were civilians who found apartments in the same building as Agent Jacobsen or very nearby. The ability to occupy those apartments was related to the availability of sufficient funds to overpay landlords who were easily led to the conclusion that it would be an unsound policy economically to spread abroad information about their recent windfalls.

The first thing Ivory's agents learned that was of red-flag significance was that Jacobsen had a girl-friend—Anna-Marie Jessen—and that she lived in a large and well-appointed apartment in Jacobsen's building. She fit the description of a 'trophy girl-friend' in every respect: she was very well-dressed, had no visible means of support, and spent her days in spas and her evenings in clubs.

Two Crip women obtained employment in businesses regularly frequented by Anna-Marie including one who was hired as a masseuse in the New York Uppity Spa which Anna-Marie preferred. The other became Anna-Marie's regular manicurist and pedicurist in her favorite nail salon, Tootsies. The two Crip women were very good at what they did and soon gathered a clientele from the top tier of the social register; and because they were not averse to a little snooping, they were able to riffle through their clients' purses and to obtain a wealth of information from all of them. None of them seemed to have anything to do with Anna-Marie except for the coincidence that they had the same manicurist and pedicurist. Anna-Marie's driver's license, club ID cards, social security numbers and banking information, however, proved to be illuminating. It seems that pretty Anna-Marie Jessen was a very rich young woman, very rich indeed. For a girl who was unemployed and did not seem to be the owner of any kind of business, she had done very well for herself.

Mac's team in Virginia made some headway as well, after a delay in start-up. Three names surfaced: Abner Christiansen worked as a cryptanalyst for the NSA Data Center—code named Bumblehive—a 1.5 billion-dollar, one million square-foot complex in obscure Bluffdale / Camp Williams LEED Silver facility, Utah—the first IC CNCI [Intelligence Community Comprehensive National Cyber-security Initiative] center for the NSA. His name surfaced because he had frequent cell phone contact with two members of the Kosher Nostra [Israeli organized crime syndicate] in Tel Aviv. The gangsters were Abraham Kosneski and Milton Cohen, both high-ranking and with ties to the Russian mafia. In and of itself, that would have been worrisome; but what alerted Mac's team, was that the Russian mafia gangsters were on the no-fly list because of known funds transfers to al Qaeda front charities.

Gwendolyn Nielson worked at the CIA Middle-East desk as an analyst. She had a drug problem—heroin—and was in hawk to her gills with loan sharks from the Cosa Nostra Delissiano family. Again, that would have been unacceptable to the CIA; but the reasons Nielson's name rose to the attention of Mac's group was because she did not seem to have to pay down on her account. The principle in the account rose almost exponentially due to the flagrantly high interest rate she was paying.

The third name to surface was that of Mark M. Sharron. The researchers in Virginia learned that the name was false and that much of what Mark had included in his application and registration as a DARPA [Defense Advanced Research Projects Agency] analyst was false—not flagrantly so, but in many pertinent and telling details. First of all, his name was not real. Muntisir Muhammad Shamon had entered the United States on a Pakistani passport in 1998 and sometime thereafter morphed into Mark M. Sharron. Shamon had relatives in the mountainous region of North Waziristan and South Waziristan with long-standing ties to the Taliban and who had been known to harbor Usama bin Laden during his long effort to escape U.S. justice.

Both Mac and McGee agreed that the three should be put under the closest scrutiny and also that the best organizations to perform the day-to-day work should come from the intelligence services of the NYPD, the LAPD, and the CPD in order to avoid any indication that the federal intelligence services were interested. Sybil agreed and a month long search of every aspect of the three persons of interest commenced.

Otherwise, even after nearly 30,000 subjects were evaluated or questioned or surveilled, no other likely candidates emerged as being suspicious enough to be considered to be the mole. Three months of searching were reduced down to a multi-law enforcement project to find out which, if any, of the four suspects was the mole. Hundreds of individuals were found to have some peccadillo or other, to have committed petty crimes, or communicated with dubious sources outside the country.

Sybil re-interviewed the directors of the intelligence services, including the military officers after they had all gone through vetting by polygraph. Not one of them failed the lie-detector test, but Sybil concentrated on the DCIA Martin Edelweiss because of his apparent evasive maneuvers during his original interview.

Sybil	DCIA
Good morning, Director.	—Good morning, Gideon. Let's make this brief. I'm busy.
I have only a few questions, and they are based on your answers during the last interview and upon your polygraph results.	—I passed the test.
You have resources you should not have accessed for your personal benefit.	—I don't know who you are, but I am certain that you do not outrank me.
That is both true and irrelevant. What is relevant is the evidence that you utilized several old tried and true evade and deceive methods during the interview, but not in the polygraph. Please explain.	—It was a matter of habit. I always chew my cheek, take half a valium, and put a thumb tack in my shoe before taking the polygraph test. I wanted to see if you would catch me. During the polygraph, I told the strict truth and did not feel any need to use the methods of deception. I am pleased, frankly, that you were so observant during the interview.
Well, Director, you are off the hook. We are making good progress. You can share that with POTUS during today's PDB.	—I will, Gideon. Keep up the good work, but know that we can't take forever.
I am well aware.	—Keep me posted as best you can.

Chapter Six

Sybil and Mac traveled separately to Utah and found a no-name motel in Bluffdale, just outside Salt Lake City. Sybil arrived first and set up in the bedroom with her voice distorter and in disguise to preserve her anonymity. There, they met with the surveillance team that had been tailing Abner Christiansen.

Mac had his three investigators sit in the uncomfortable furniture in the main room of the suite.

Sybil asked—in her best impression of Donald Duck—"Anything new since yesterday?"

"Nothing."

"What does the guy do? He doesn't seem to have a family or a social life. Have you seen any coincidental repeat meetings? Any recurrent faces?"

"Sorry, no. Aside from his fairly frequent cell phone calls to a couple of Israeli thugs and another two Russian *mafiya*—which you know about—he is as predictable and blah as the desert sand out here. Eats in the same places, watches lots of TV—mostly re-runs of *Perry Mason, I Love Lucy,* and *Barney*

Fife in Podunk—and spends boocoo time on the computer, hikes the same monotonous ten mile long trail five days a week, and goes out to a rare movie—always at the Bluffdale Megaplex theaters. He likes oldies but goodies, and nothing rated higher than PG. He is the very picture of boring and unthreatening. His past history is just as colorless. High school was straight "A"s, no girl-friend, no buddies, no sports. Same thing in college; he graduated in the top ten from Cal Tech, never joined anything—not even the math club—never had so much as a parking ticket. As he did in childhood and high school, he doesn't do religion or humanitarian service."

"Have you gotten to his computer?"

"We know everything he has ever done on his NSA computer, compliments of the DNSA. Nothing."

"Any idea what his communications with cell phone contact with two members of the Kosher Nostra in Tel Aviv—Abraham Kosneski and Milton Cohen and the *mafiya* are about?" Sybil asked.

"Only that the Israelis are both high-ranking members of an international crime syndicate and the Russian mafias are equally unkosher, nothing. It's not a crime to talk, and nothing we've learned indicates that the man is otherwise involved in their activities. We don't like it any better than you do, but he personally is not linked to the al Qaeda front charities, just his Russian pals. There are no grounds for a warrant, and certainly nothing that would make it reasonable to arrest the man.

"What about his personal computer?"

"Can't get into it. He appears to have a uniquely personal encryption coding, and we cannot crack that without having the machine itself."

"Sounds like a little B&E is in order," Sybil and Mac said almost at the same time.

"Don't you need a warrant?" the lead investigator asked.

"Nope," Sybil said.

"I'll get NSA security in there tonight," Mac said.

"There can't be any hint of our foot prints in this escapade," Sybil said.

"The NSA guys are experts at this. They are in everybody's business all the time. Hey Gideon, do you know what a giant is?"

"I'll bite, what?"

"That's someone who goes around with his business in everybody's nose. Do you know what a dwarf is?"

"So, what is a dwarf?"

"A dwarf is like the NSA. Goes around with his nose in everybody's business."

"Fortunately, for us, that is exactly what we need tonight. I need to maintain my cover; so, you go in with them, Mac."

"No problem, Gideon. All right you guys, let's get together a team."

He and the NSA investigators left Sybil to fret while they set up the break-in. The team included the most serious computer experts in the world. It was overkill, as it turned out.

Mac entered Christiansen's room first. The team could hear him softly snoring in his bed. Mac padded silently to where Christiansen lay supine with only his noisy breathing to indicate that he was alive. Mac opened his back pack and pulled out a small aerosol can. He pressed the nozzle and emitted two spritzes of chloroform in ulta-fine droplets over the sleeping man's face. The only change was less snoring, indicative of a deeper level of sleep.

The NSA security agents moved into high gear. They dismantled Christiansen's computer and fiddled with a few electronic wires then downloaded the entirety of their victim's hard-drive onto a separate hard-drive that they had in their backpacks. The process of the data transfer took four minutes. The entire elapsed time from their entry into the house until they had the computer put back together and walked out the door was fourteen minutes, thirty-six seconds.

Mac asked, "Will he be able to tell that his computer has been tampered with?"

"No. We changed nothing. What we did leaves no more trail than if we had been able to take what we wanted with a thumb drive."

"How long do you think it will take to crack the encryption code?"

"Depends. Is it a direct code or a serially rotating encryption which changes daily, hourly, or even by the minute? That takes some doing, and I doubt that he went to all of that trouble for his personal stuff. We'll see. The analysts and code-breakers will get on it tonight."

"Thanks. You do good work."

The two agents nodded and smiled.

Anna-Marie Jessen was unaware that her computer had been hacked and that the CIA, NSA, and a private investigative team knew everything there was to know about her personal accounts—her personal fortune—except the source of the money. There had been no withdrawals on record. Although Anna-Marie lived the life of a high maintenance generously kept woman, the money did not seem to be coming from her account. The intelligence and law enforcement agencies could not—for all of their efforts—find anything illegal, although they were certain that there was something rotten in Denmark. She had no known associates in the underworld or among terrorists. She had never traveled to any of the U.S. borders or coasts. Her boyfriend also had a clean record and was highly regarded at work. The investigators drew a blank.

That was not the case with NCIS Special Agent Myron Jacobsen's finances. It was his money, and he watched over it with all the care of a mother humming bird tending her nest full of miniscule eggs. He had every reason to trust Anna-Marie, who, after all, was enjoying a life of rich leisure and had to do nothing but make him happy a few nights a week and to allow him full access to and use of her bank account. But, Myron Jacobsen grew up in Montana and early in life learned the first lesson about being a rancher—trust everyone but brand your cattle. He received regular account reports from his bank and Anna-Marie's to his iPhone like everybody else; but, in addition, he could obtain an immediate record of any electronic activity occurring in the account. He had an app for that and visited it twice daily.

He was puzzled to find electronic tracks in recent reports that indicated that the account had been hacked, but nothing transferred or stolen. His immediate knee-jerk reaction was that the account was being electronically monitored by the IRS. His second reaction was to contact his superior in Washington, D.C.

Gwendolyn Nielson began drinking after the second visit from the Soriano set of the Delissiano family. They painted her a very ugly picture of what would happen if she failed to make payment in full, including interest, before the end of the month. To punctuate their demands the three men sent by Miguel Soriano raped Gwendolyn mercilessly.

Guido Musalla left her room. His parting threat was, "We know where you work. We won't kill you or break your knees. We'll just be little birdies who let your bosses at the CIA know about your financial problems that come from your nasty little drug habit. You've been warned."

For Gwendolyn, the question became, "which threat is the worst—the loan sharks or the CIA?" One would think she would be scared straight and stop her frenetic gambling. The only thing that curbed her losses at all was that she could no longer afford to travel to Atlantic City, let alone to continue her monthly trips to Las Vegas. Her first solution was to drink more. That led to absenteeism from her analyst's desk at Langley. And that brought her to the attention of her supervisors. When they reported her erratic behavior and declining work output to HR, the Gideon group obtained a report. Then, Gwendolyn Nielson's problems began to get serious.

Mark M. Sharron, aka Muntisir Muhammad Shamon was tailed 24/7. His land-line and cellular telephone, e-mail, and postal communications were all scrutinized by hostile experts looking for a clue that he was dirty. He had committed cardinal sins by DARPA standards by faking his name and other information submitted to the government agency when he applied. He had lied by omission when he failed to report the details of his family's connections to the Taliban and to al Qaeda. That was enough to get him fired, but not enough to have the government have him formally arrested. There was certainly not enough evidence to bring him to trial. Even the most zealous federal prosecutor would not pursue the case given the huge back load of more serious cases. It was, however, enough to pique the interest of Gideon.

Five months had passed, and only fourteen individuals evaluated in the mole hunt had been suspicious enough to result in extensive questioning by the group. Of them four were fired without explanation; two underwent unproductive 'enhanced interrogation'; and seven where detained in comfortable quarters at the nation's preeminent center for information, intelligence and cyber analysis and cyber counter-terrorism, the United States Army Garrison, at Fort George G. Meade, Maryland. The detention was for the duration of the mole hunt.

As draconian and unfair as all of that seemed to be, it was of very little value towards the solution of the problem: there is a mole in the intelligence services, and the Gideon group assigned to ferret the traitor out has only three real suspects and no concrete evidence.

NCIS Special Agent Myron Jacobsen arranged with his superior officer to meet in a dark and run-down bar in Washington Highlands, which is a large residential neighborhood in Southeast Washington, D.C. It is the largest residential neighborhood in Ward 8—the poorest and least developed section of Washington—and very few businesses prosper there. The Devil's Bar was not one of the prosperous ones, and the neighborhood was one of those even the cops would not enter at night. As a result, it was the perfect place for a meet. There was almost no traffic on the rundown streets. Only two vehicles—both more than twenty years old—were parked in proximity to the bar. Jacobsen saw three pedestrians within four blocks of the bar, and all of them were old black people scurrying to get back to their apartments and off the mean streets. A bum was lying in the alley beside the bar. When Jacobsen passed him (or her?), he could not be sure if the lump of rags was dead or just sleeping off a bad drunk.

He sat in a back corner booth next to the entry into the small grill area. It was after midnight, and there were no customers in the bar who were interested in food. The food had a well-deserved reputation as being execrable and consisting largely of re-used grease even during the day. He fidgeted in his slick vinyl seat and kept his hands off the table for fear of contamination. Where was the boss?

Ivory White and two of his homies drove slowly passed the Devils Bar and noted that Special Agent Jacobsen's rental car—a used Ford coupe—was parked so that it blocked entry into the alley. It had been no great feat of surveillance to locate the vehicle. Ivory had followed the NCIS agent to the Livingston Road Used Car Rental lot by the Acme Liquor Store in Oxon Hill, Maryland. Jacobsen's personal car had a GPS device attached to its rear axle mount, and Ivory and his men followed him from his apartment outside of Quantico to Oxon Hill. Dwight 'Inky' Foster, one of Ivory's most trusted homies and by far the best actor, detained Jacobsen after he paid the $9.99 three-day weekend rental special reservation fee for his car. Inky was good at playing a panhandling drunk and even got a buck from Jacobsen to get him to go away. While that transaction was taking place, Ivory rolled under the rental car and placed a tracking device in the right rear wheel well.

Ivory watched Jacobsen circle the bar three times making his destination apparent. Melvin 'Deek the Sneak' Bradshaw—another useful homie of Ivory's—took his rag collection and stretched out in the alley next to the bar. Ivory and a somewhat cleaned up Inky entered the establishment and sat on bar stools in the dim light near the rest room. They paid no attention to Special Agent Jacobsen when he entered, scrutinized Ivory, Deek, and two tired working girls who were seated in a booth three spots down the aisle from the place he selected to sit and wait for his boss.

It was after one when the door to the Devils Bar opened again. A tall man in a black hoody under a dark trench coat and jeans walked in and wasted no time in taking a seat opposite to Jacobsen. Ivory trained his cell phone in the direction of the two men in the booth. It was equipped with a high-tech phone GSM Bug Spy Listening Device which allowed him to listen to the two as they spoke in soft tones and to record everything they said with nothing short of amazing clarity. He was also able to get two photos of the face of Jacobsen's visitor—one frontal and one in profile.

The conversation was engrossing, even though—or maybe because—it was stilted and phrased in cautious coded language.

"You took your sweet time, getting here, boss. Any problems?"

"No, just craft. Didn't want to have company."

"Anything?"

"No. This is not my first rodeo, probby."

"So, whatta you think about my info?"

"Trouble. I'll check on the tax angle, but we can't take chances or have loose ends. *Capiche?*"

"Let me be sure, here. You want to take her on a vacation?"

"She deserves it. Make it a real long one."

"I'm a little nervous. Maybe it's time for me to see new places."

"Maybe so, but only on official assignment. You're too valuable to leave your employment just yet. We have obligations, remember? The other people in the contract are not likely to be happy about an interruption in the delivery of service. Get me?"

"I do. But I'm still concerned."

"Noted."

While the two men were talking, Deek left his nice soft resting place on the filthy concrete of the alley and went out in search of the visitor's car. It was ridiculously easy to find. Two blocks away in a trash strewn alley, Deek found a sleek, shiny, clean Suburban with federal government plates. He put a GPS tracker in the wheel well. Before he could break into the large vehicle for a look-around, he heard footsteps. They were close; so, he rolled behind a row of discarded boxes piled two high, drew his 9 mm, and waited silently in the darkness.

The man in black from the Devils Bar strode quickly to the car. Although Deek could not see his face, he could make a judgment about him: the ramrod stiff bearing, focus, and wariness equaled military. Deek waited until the Suburban drove away before dusting himself off and making his way back to the bar. He passed the used rental car he knew was being used by the NCIS agent just as the man got in. Neither man paid the other any attention.

Ivory, Inky, and Deek left the bar but waited for half an hour before deciding that it was safe to get back into their own car and to go disturb McGee. It was 4:15 when Ivory connected with McGee on his cell phone.

"What do you have, Ivory?"

"Serious stuff. I think it's enough to get Gideon and his Donald Duck talk and Mac Young together with us. We have a couple of photos and a recording. Deek has a serious piece of intel which we shouldn't talk about on the phone."

"Gotcha. Good work as usual, Ivory. Come by my place; and in the meantime, I'll get hold of Gideon and Mac. We are probably going to have to meet at Langley. Oh, I presume you kept a tail on Jacobsen."

"Sure. Two of my guys are on him. They tell me that he is headed in the direction of his apartment. He's had a long night."

"Good. I'll see you at the office."

Sybil was asleep on her king-size bed with Charles. Cerisse had sneaked into bed with her parents after having a nightmare. Nightmares were very much a part of the residual PTSD from her life as a slave in the Congo. She was doing well on low doses of clonazepam, olanzapine, and propranolol for her recurring anxiety; but the nightmares still intruded. Sybil's Gideon mobile phone vibrated against her hand under her pillow. She was instantly awake, a holdover from her neurosurgery residency and early practice days. She slipped out of bed and softly walked into the hall outside the large bedroom.

McGee gave his code, and Sybil answered with hers.

"Are you on a secure line?" she asked.

"I am. We have news that won't keep. Let's meet at the OHB in an hour. I'll take our corporate jet up. I have already contacted Young. I think we have just stepped on a hornet's nest."

"I'll be there," she said and hung up.

Mac and the civilians, McGee, White, Bradshaw, and Foster met on the front stairs of the OHB. Sybil came separately.

Chapter Seven

Abner Christiansen, trusted NSA analyst, awakened more refreshed than he could ever remember. He had not taken a sleeping pill, but he was sure that he had not moved all night. He had some Costco Premium Chocolate drink and a piece of whole wheat toast. He felt positively healthy as he got into his Chevy and headed to the NSA Bumblehive to start his fascinating day analyzing calls coming from the financial district in San Francisco that had been flagged because of the use of keywords—al Qaeda, bomb, kill, terminate, target, airport, airplane, subway, train, drone, etc. His real job—as he now had come to understand it—was to clear all of those innocent calls; so, the NSA could breathe easy and let the callers stay blissfully unaware that they were being monitored every day. It was going to be another day like all of the other days at his job and in his life.

He laughed to himself as he mocked his existence, "*I have job. I go to work every day. After work, I come home. I eat; I watch T.V. and then go to bed. On the weekends, I don't do nothin'. On Monday, my routine starts again. No worries.*"

Abner Christiansen could not have been more wrong.

Three NSA cryptanalysts, working in the same building—the Bumblehive—were able to crack Abner's seemingly impenetrable code after only two hours of work. In fact, the code was not all that sophisticated or complex. It was a book cipher. Among the books photographed by infrared photography in Abner's room was *Lolita*, by Vladimir Nabokov. It was the only fictional work on Abner's shelves which were stacked at random with math and encryption non-fiction—very professional and related to his work. Since his computer at work contained only information strictly related to his ongoing work, the cryptanalysts, thought there was a chance that it was indeed a book cipher based on *Lolita*. It was not quite that simple. The word "Lolita" did not immediately serve as a password. One of the cryptanalysts, when he saw the photograph of the hard bound copy of Lolita, started humming *Thank Heaven for Little Girls*, the old Maurice Chevalier song from the '50s as a joke.

One of his colleagues had a moment of inspiration. They got onto the internet and looked up the lyrics. They then tried a systematic inclusion of lyrics fragments as possible passwords. Serendipity struck two of the three analysts.

"Maybe he's a pedophile," they said at once.

"So let's try, 'For without them, what would little boys do?'" their partner suggested.

It didn't work.

"Too long."

"Try 'withoutthemwhatwouldlittleboysdo'?'"

Still didn't work.

Finally, they put in the year—1958—when Chevalier first published the song.

That didn't work, either, but 1957, when he wrote the song, finally did work. They finally entered 1957whatwouldlittleboysdo.

Bingo.

The hard drive opened. The desktop screen saver was a high resolution photograph of the Statue of Liberty. There were only eight desk top icons. All of them were opened and proved useless. The cryptanalysts had a good group sigh and were about to admit that it had been a clever but futile idea. Then one of them took a harder look at the Statue of Liberty. In the photograph was a small rectangle that looked like a "Keep-off-the-Grass" sign although it was not possible to make out details of the possible writing.

"Check out a picture of the Statue of Liberty. I want to make a comparison."

They looked up Statue of Liberty images on Google. None of them showed that apparently innocuous rectangle.

"Let's have a better looked at this…" he pointed to the rectangle.

He left-clicked on it, and nothing happened. When it opened up with a right click, a catalogue of icons up loaded to the file. The cryptanalysts then found a complete copy of Lolita on-line and applied their international anti-terrorism software to find out how to bring up the actual data or photographs. A block cipher is only suitable for the secure cryptographic transformation—encryption or decryption—of one fixed-length group of bits called a block. Shortly, the algorithm that Christiansen used was revealed to his competing NSA analysts as the mode of finding the correct phrases. After that it was simple, because Christiansen had an orderly mind. He went page by page in the book selecting the last sentence or sentence fragment to identify each file in the large folder and gave it a harmless picture icon—flowers and cuddly little animals. It took nearly twenty minutes for all of the small photo icons to become activated. It only took a double click on one of them to answer the questions about the eccentricities of their fellow NSA analyst, Abner Christiansen. That small icon opened to 100 flagrantly pornographic images of children.

One of the cryptanalysts, a father of three little girls, gagged and turned his head away.

"Lord in Heaven," he exclaimed, "I have only heard of this kind of stuff. I will never be able to get these pictures out of my mind."

They picked icons at random and found digital photos, movie clips, and circular playback streamers. The content included S&M, adult males with young females, adult females with young males, young males and females, young females and females and vice versa, and bestiality. You name it; it was there. All of the crypanalysts took a shower before they contacted the Gideon group who had brought the hard drive to them.

They explained what they found and how they found it.

"What do we do next?"

"Just hold on to the evidence. We'll send a guy to pick it up. Can you put it on a flash drive?"

"It'll take two, maybe even three. There's a ton of stuff on this site."

"Splurge. We can afford it. You keep the hard drive itself, and we'll take the thumb drives for now. The cops will want the hard drive, I'm sure. You can tell them that you found it on routine check of NSA employee computers or whatever comes to mind, but don't say a thing about us, okay?"

"Sure."

The CIA assistant to Mac then called Mac on his secure mobile phone. Mac was just going into a meeting at CIA headquarters. The conversation was brief. Mac called the Bluffdale Police Department and reported the finding of the child pornography site and arranged for the lead detective to meet a NSA security officer in the local Denny's for the hand over.

Mac, and the civilians, McGee, White, Bradshaw, and Foster walked up the front stairs of the OHB and were processed to be able to go to the seventh floor to the secure interview room. Once in the room, Mac let everyone know that they could cross Abner Christiansen off their list for all practical purposes. For certain it would be decades before he was ever allowed to get near a phone or a computer again. Of course, his relationships to the Russian mobsters would have to be more fully investigated; but, based on the evidence thus far of secrets and a huge scandal, and lack of evidence of him being a traitor, they were all sure he was not their man. He could well be a purveyor of child pornography, but there was nothing to indicate that he was a spy or that he divulged the secrets he gleaned from his top-secret work.

The room was set up with all they needed. McGee provided the two photos taken by Ivory White, and they were put into the facial recognition equipment—the FBI's 'bigger, faster and better' NGI [Next Generation Identification] biometrics system. In 2015, the recognition process had matured into a science of sophisticated mathematical representations and matching processes. The Suburban's federal license plate was run through the system. Both the car and the man in the photograph were so well known that it took only a few minutes to find matches. The matches belonged to each other. The face in the photo was that of Vice-Admiral Duncan Lloyd Jennings, DCNO [Deputy Chief of Naval Operations—the N2/N6 and the DNI (Director of Naval Intelligence)]. There are four DCNOs second in command to the four-star admiral who directs all naval operations and who answers to the CJCS [Chairman of the Joint Chiefs of Staff] and to the president.

Each of the agents looking at the results had thought himself or herself to be immune to being stunned, but they were wrong. This could not be. There had to be a mistake.

"I have to let POTUS know right now. Maybe there's an explanation, but I can't think of anything but the obvious," said a much sobered Sybil in her Donald Duck voice.

Mac said, "Okay, Gideon. We'll get every bit of information we can. Maybe it is really nothing. Maybe our other persons of interest are involved and maybe not, and maybe there are still one or more unsubs out there. Our work is not done."

"Indeed," said Sybil.

Sybil called the president on her secure phone.

The president said, "NI One. This is a secure phone. Who is speaking?"

"S7A3N0D75#Marburg communicating under ultra TS/SCI code established by PDD-3071."

"Gideon?"

"Yes, Sir. We've had a break-through. However, we have more investigation to do before we can say for sure that we have our guys—as it turns out. Just how many may be involved is uncertain now. But here is what we have. Hold on to your seat, NI One."

She presented her evidence as succinctly but completely as she could.

"Vice-Admiral Jennings!?" I see him at least once a week. He has an impeccable record. He is a genuine American hero."

"And maybe a genuine American traitor and spy. Don't forget Benedict Arnold, Kim Philby in Great Britain, John Anthony Walker Jr., a U. S. Navy officer, and Robert Hansson, the pure as the driven snow Mormon FBI traitor. The evidence is damning, but we need to keep a lid on it for now. I am sure you will want to inform the CNO, but caution him not to do anything that would alert Adm. Jennings until we can get all the information necessary to nail him and any co-conspirators."

President Willets had his appointment secretary pencil in the CNO, Admiral Craigmont Dorrity for eleven-thirty.

The president met the admiral at the entry door into the Oval Office.

"Good morning, Mr. President. What can I do for you?"

"I am glad to get right down to business. It is what the two of us can do together. I will give you some ultra top-secret information—your eyes and ears only along with mine first, then we need to brainstorm some."

"A navy problem, I presume?"

"Very much so, and also an intelligence community and a national security issue."

President Willets gave Adm. Dorrity the short version of the involvement of his DCNO, Vice-Admiral Duncan Lloyd Jennings, in what could be espionage and murder of four top-secret intelligence agents. Only someone with access to highly classified information could have given away or sold our vital information and callously assisted al Qaeda in their assassinations.

"Admiral. We need to keep this close to our vests, but we need to prevent anything going from Admiral Jennings's office to any unauthorized recipient. Early on, we have to keep it secret until the elite committee I have organized to find our mole has a chance to get enough evidence to prosecute."

"The intelligence services have their own ways of dealing with traitors, Mr. President. I am almost certain that if Jennings—I can't bear to call him, admiral—is the culprit and if we start bugging his phones or computers, he will catch it immediately. He is trained to do that. It is his business as the DNI. I think he will be in the wind if he gets even a whiff of smoke from our investigation."

"Can you give him an assignment that will fence him in until our committee can finish its work?"

"I can figure out a way to put him on a ship, and I can have a couple of SEALS or good master chiefs watch him to prevent him hiding or getting off. Do you have any ideas of what would be so important that a vice-admiral of intelligence operations should be aboard a ship?"

"Not off-hand, Admiral; but I have an extremely resourceful team working on the problem of the mole. The leader is someone nobody would suspect is in that position, and I believe we can come up with a solution. It'll have to be quick, and that probably is an advantage. We need to come up with a serious and secret intelligence threat and get our man on board the *Eisenhower* or some other ship worthy of having a DCNO aboard. So, why don't you come up with the ship by two this afternoon. I will meet with my team—they operate under the code name of Gideon, incidentally—and come up with an emergency that puts him at sea."

"Aye, aye, Sir!" the CNO told the Commander-in-Chief.

Chapter Eight

Oval Office, White House, Washington, D.C., 1320
Present: POTUS, DCIA, DDDIA, NSA, CNO, DCIA-CT,
and DUSCYBERCOM, Sybil Norcroft and Mac Young,
Special Agents of the CIA
Re: Operational plan for mission code name Gideon

The president explained the problem—how to get Vice-Admiral Jennings to board a secure U.S. ship of the line on a pretext that he would believe. He also explained the logistical difficulties.

"Mac and Sybil, can you two communicate quickly enough with Gideon to get the investigative and analysis work done in the next few days?"

It was more than a little weird to have to pretend that she was not Gideon, and that she would be talking to herself shortly.

She answered with a perfectly straight face, "Yes, Mr. President. However, there is no guarantee that we can produce enough evidence for a court, including for a court martial proceeding."

Mac said what need to be said, "Mr. President, lady and gentlemen, we have an extraordinarily sensitive problem on our hands. Our first imperative must be to secure our nation's vital secrets. We must place the admiral under arrest and get him to a secure location before he can bolt or dump a load of crucial information into the al Qaeda pipeline. That trumps the need for attention to prissy legal details from the way I see it. I am sure that Special Agent Norcroft agrees."

She nodded her assent.

"Have you come up with a plausible excuse to get Jennings on board a ship of the line, Adm. Dorrity?"

"Nothing very satisfactory. For one thing, however plausible our excuse may seem, we will have to seclude him from his communications network. He is no dummy. He will catch on as soon as he is unable to get into his network."

Sybil raised her hand.

"Dr. Norcroft?" President Willets said. "Have an idea?"

"What if we feed Jennings information that is probably not unknown to him already. We can tell him that one of the CIA's most secret agents is on the ship…"

"The *Dwight D. Eisenhower*," Adm. Dorrity said.

"Okay. And we have intel that indicates that there is a mole on the ship about whom there is mounting evidence that he or she is the assassin who murdered our CIA agents, and he or she plans to kill the rogue agent and to obtain the intelligence material the agent is trying to get out to his spymasters. He carries the information in an implanted chip, and we need to get to him before the assassin does. We don't know what his alias is on board the ship, but he or she is willing to convey the information to an officer of the standing of

Adm. Jennings. The information is so secret that only a very senior officer with an Ultra TS/SCI clearance rating with SSBI rating can be allowed to handle it. The security of the admiral's communication system aboard the ship would help to guarantee the safety of transmission of the data from our agent to the CNO and DCIA. I propose that we sweeten the pot by having SSG-CNO Captain Victor Raylan and DCIA-CT Coxworthy here accompany Jennings."

The DCIA had been listening closely, "I think it's as good a plan as any. I would like to add a couple of wrinkles. One is to have some sort of phony temporary communications failure aboard the *Eisenhower*. That way Jennings is less likely to suspect that he is being had because he can't get information in or out, and neither can anyone else. It isolates him from his network. The other wrinkle is to throw in a diversion—something that will disrupt the usual ship routine enough to throw him off."

President Willets asked, "Director Edelweiss, anything to add or subtract from Dr. Norcroft's suggested plan?"

"No, I like it in principle. It will take a bit to get the whole thing together. I would like to suggest that our Dr. Norcroft provide the diversion. She is attractive, brilliant, and an exciting speaker. She has the built in admiration and name-recognition of being the darling of Wolf News—a well-known celebrity. I think she can charm the pants off Jennings…figuratively speaking, of course."

He flashed a brief mischievous grin at Sybil, who rolled her eyes.

"And Sybil has a pretty significant record as a field officer. She is resourceful and some movie superhero qualities, and she can defend herself. She is not above getting a little blood on her hands," the president offered.

Sybil blushed.

"We could drop an ever so subtle hint that maybe, just maybe, Sybil could be the secret agent who has come aboard to receive the intel from our fictitious undercover agent," DCIA Edelweiss added.

"Sybil, you up for it?"

"I suppose so. I hope I'm enough of a believable femme fatale to pull it off."

"I'm convinced about that," DCIA-CT Roland LaStarza said with an appreciative grin that made everyone laugh, but no one doubted the accuracy of his observation.

LaStarza was a man from whom secrets could only be pried by the use of surgical instruments on his anesthetized body, but this was the time and the place to divulge one.

"Mr. President, lady and gentlemen, we actually have an undercover agent on board the *Dwight D. Eisenhower*, one that may be already suspected by Adm. Jennings. He is a Special Agent of the NCIS and is on board incognito. He has a top-secret clearance but not an ultra top-secret one. I'm not sure he would have come into Jennings's radar field by name, but his mission should at least be known in the DNI files. He is expected to convey information about a drug smuggling ring to an intelligence agent whom he does not yet know. I can let our receiving agent know that he is to back off, and let our undercover agent know about Dr. Norcroft."

"That's all right, but Jennings will have to be informed that something is going on; so, he will make a play to get her alone to obtain her information."

"If we go that route, Dr. Norcroft will have to be under surveillance by selected security personnel from the intelligence department on board the ship 24/7. There cannot be a slip-up that imperils Dr. Norcroft or this mission to trap Jennings," said the DCIA.

"We'll get it worked out by the time she gets on the ship," DCIA-CT LaStarza said.

Sybil sent McGee after two of the remaining suspects, Mark Sharron and Gwendolyn Nielson. She gave him detain and arrest authority. Mac Young and his team were to concentrate on NCIS Special Agent Myron Jacobsen. Jacobsen was very much a time sensitive suspect, and it was time to pull out the stops. Mac and his team left for Quantico to arrest him either at work or at his apartment between the Quantico Marine Base and Fort Meade. Three additional agents were sent to arrest Anna-Marie Jessen. A quick call to McGee's two employees in Tootsie's manicure and pedicure parlor indicated that she had not been in the establishment for two days. Presumably she was at home. Since she and her boyfriend Myron lived in the same building, the agents hoped they could make it a twofer.

The agents sent after Anna-Marie did not find her at home; so, they picked her locks and walked in. The closets were largely empty of clothing, and her bathroom had been denuded of cosmetics, medications, and her entry closet was missing her luggage. All of her IDs—passport, driver license, and pass cards for her bank were gone. It was apparent that the young woman had left for a spur-of-the moment vacation, or she was in the wind. Agent Dunlevey texted that information to Mac Young immediately.

Mac's heart quickened.

"Let's move it, guys. The girl friend has taken off, it looks like. Get the watchers on the speaker phone who were on his tail for the last two days. If you pray, say one to whoever that he has not gotten wind of us and taken off."

Nobody's prayer was answered. The agents were breathless having spent a frantic morning trying to locate the NCIS agent.

Agent Hinckley reported what he knew, "Looks like our perp has gone on a camping trip. We saw him carry a huge ballistic nylon bag, fishing poles, a couple of rifles, a tent, a backpack, and a large box of food. It took him about four trips to get it all into the trunk of his car. We set out after him, but he must have lost us either intentionally or maybe just in the traffic."

"I have a bad feeling about this," Mac said. "Don't we still have the GPS tracker on him?"

"We do, but it isn't working."

"Disabled or discarded," Mac said. "Get hold of Quantico and get a couple of FBI helicopters in the air with a description of his car. Put out a BOLO on him. He's on the run, and we need everything available to get him. Call the marshal's service."

"I have a worse feeling," Agent Caruthers, one of the men who had been sent to arrest Anna-Marie said, "it could be possible that the big nylon bag had Anna-Marie's body in it, and Jacobsen is on the run. What would you like to bet on how much money is left in Anna-Marie's account?"

The team was grim-faced and angry. Now, about all they could do was sit on their hands and wait until something happened to give them a place to go. Mac called Sybil and let her know the bad news. She contacted the DCIA and the president. The president told her to alert law-enforcement and ICE to consider Jacobsen Public Enemy Number One. Then, they all sat and waited.

FBI forensic accounting called with the news everyone dreaded but expected. All of Anna-Marie's money had been transferred to an off-shore numbered account in the Reserve Bank of Vanuatu. Vanuatu is the least friendly banking country in the world for U.S. and European governments which is a source of booming economy for the tiny island country.

"We'll never see a dime of that money," Mac said. "They jail FBI agents for thirty years if they ask a lot of questions about the accounts of any individual or company."

"Then, we'll just have to see to it that none of them ever gets out of jail with enough brain power or years left to enjoy it," said the forensic accountant whose purpose in life was to prevent crooks from prospering.

Mark M. Sharron, aka Muntisir Muhammad Shamon, was arrested in his small office at DARPA after the morning's briefing by the chief, Col. Avery Holmes. Col. Holmes had been informed by the Gideon group before the FBI marched like a small army to Mark's office.

"Stand up," said Special Agent Grant Foster, "Muntisir Muhammad Shamon, you are under arrest for felony perjury related to your falsification of application records, functioning under an assumed name, and for treason—treating with the enemy. All of this is covered under the Patriot Act. You might want to let your lawyer know that when you finally get to see one."

"I don't know what you are talking about! I am an American citizen. I have my rights. You can't do this!"

"You are not an American citizen. You falsified your application for a visa and to obtain a green card. You never got close to being a citizen. You supplied vital information to the enemies of the United States—the Taliban—through your family in the Waziristan Autonomous Regions. Under the Patriot Act, those acts caused you to forfeit any rights you might have had as an American citizen."

The FBI agent was almost shouting. The effect of the noise, the presence of the powerful military appearing FBI SWAT team, and the information that one of their own was a spy—a traitor to the country they all loved—shocked everyone in the office into stunned silence.

Special Agent Foster jerked Muntisir up by his lapels, spun him around, and hand-cuffed his wrists behind his back— too tightly on purpose. The next stop for Muntisir was an extraordinarily secure dungeon-like set of tunnels underneath the huge Bank of America building in Washington D.C. The numbers on the elevators did not indicate the two subter- ranean rooms below the bank offices, and the rooms did not have chairs or beds. He was in for a long stay; he knew that. There was a dreadful stench in the room owing to the only toilet facility being a drain hole in the floor, and the previous inmates in the room were none too particular about tidiness.

Gwendolyn Nielson was sitting in her cubicle in the CIA overseas threat assessment office when her supervisor called her to his office.

"Gwen, what's going on? You've worked here for years and never a black mark in your record. Now, you show up late when you do show up. Your mind is not on your work, and your friends have to cover for you. You look you are in a daze." He paused, then went on, "your breath smells of alcohol. You've been drinking this morning. You know the Company will not tolerate that. The authorities have been notified."

Gwendolyn gave up and lost hope entirely. She sat as mute as a statue and waited for whatever came next.

"Gwen, by all rights, I should just let you back out onto the street; so, the nice Delissiano family folks can find you. But, I'm not like that. There's an intelligence group that wants to talk to you first. I understand they can be quite persuasive."

Gwendolyn fainted.

"Gideon, we have him in sight!" Mac shouted into the phone.

Sybil worked on her calmness qualities before answering, "Where?"

One of the fibbie helicopters spotted the car headed down the I-95. Looks like he's hell-bent to get to Miami at the moment."

"Is he speeding?"

"It falls under the legal definition of reckless driving."

"Have the county mounties pick him up. I would rather have this look like a routine traffic stop," Sybil said.

"Consider it done, boss," Mac said.

A Dade County Sheriff's Department helicopter dropped out of the sky and buzzed the speeding car pushing down ever closer until Special Agent NCIS Myron Jacobsen had to stop. Deputy Sheriff, Clint Westhouser, walked away from the chopper with his hand on his service weapon and the holster strap undone.

"Hello there, Sir. Have you any idea how fast you were going and why I stopped you?"

"Not really, officer."

"It's deputy, but I'm not fussy. You were going 135 miles per hour. That is 75 miles over the speed limit. As we say down south, 'boah you-all are in a heap of trouble'. Step out of the car and make sure I can see your hands all the time. I get real itchy when I can't."

Jacobsen knew that he had no choice, but he also knew that Adm. Jennings would get him out of it—national security trumps county rules. He did want to avoid having his trunk opened. By the time he was out of the car, three Dade County cars with flashing lights were surrounding his vehicle.

"Get on your knees."

Jacobsen complied.

"Hands behind your head, interlock your fingers. That's a good fellow."

Deputy Westhouser handcuffed him.

"Now, can I talk?" Jacobsen said.

"Talk quiet. I got a headache," Westhouser said.

"This is all a misunderstanding, Sheriff. Please check in the left jacket pocket. You'll find a cred-pac. I am an NCIS officer on assignment. I need you to release me promptly because otherwise you will be obstructing a federal officer. You can check all of that with my superior officer, Admiral Jennings. His card is in my right jacket pocket."

Westhouser checked.

"Hummh," he mouthed, not overly impressed or concerned.

His cell phone buzzed.

"Westhouser," he answered and listened for two full minutes.

"Hummh," he mouthed again, "that was interesting. Seems you are exactly what you say you are. We are all to be real patient and look up. There are going to be a couple of those big black helicopters only the feds can afford dropping out of the sky very shortly. I learned that you are a very big shot. *Very* popular. Very popular, indeed."

Chapter Nine

Nothing more was said as the two promised black MH-6 helicopters arrived and landed ostentatiously in the slow lane of the busy six lane I-95 throughway. Six men in camouflage BDUs from the CIRG [Critical Incident Response Group] and armed ready for combat alighted from the THU [Tactical Helicopter Unit/Tactical Aviation Unit].

Special Agent Denver McIntire walked up to Deputy Westhouser and said, "Nicely done, Clint. We'll take over."

"Always happy to be of service to the Fat Boys Incorporated, Denver. This here's very special agent of the NCIS Myron Jacobsen; says so in his creds."

McIntire took the cred pack and the prisoner into custody.

"Let's open the trunk and see what secrets and scandals there might be there."

He opened the driver's side door and removed the keys. His team members put Jacobsen on the ground and stood over him while McIntire opened the trunk.

"Oh, fudge," he said—he had been practicing cleaning up his language.

There, securely wrapped in heavy ply plastic sheeting was a body. The agents unwrapped the corpse and established that it was the beautiful Anna-Marie Jessen still in rigor mortis. He snapped several photographs of the trunk, the body, and the NCIS agent and forwarded them to the FBI and to the Gideon committee. The team collected several boxes containing cash, fake IDs, and top-secret files.

"There's more to this than meets the eye," Jacobsen said. "I demand that you contact DCNO Vice-Admiral Duncan Lloyd Jennings immediately. He can clear all of this up. I am on assignment for the NCIS. If you have to, you can get hold of SecNav, too."

"We most certainly will, Mr. Jacobsen. "That is one thing you can count on. Okay, Denver, it has been the usual pleasure, but we have to get back to D.C. Mr. Jacobsen is going to answer a lot of questions."

The three individuals apprehended that day became the property of the Gideon unit and were taken to what the CIA likes to call "an undisclosed location." The location was in Loudoun County, Virginia; and it was fully prepared to receive the prisoners. So far as the rest of the world was concerned, the three simply vanished.

Sybil ordered that they all be treated respectfully and put on 24/7 suicide and security watch.

"I don't want anyone to talk to them until after we deal with the big fish in this operation, understood?"

"Yes, Sir," the guards and agents said to the Humphrey Bogart voice on the phone.

Sybil called the CNO's office, and her use of the magic word, "Gideon" granted her immediate access to Admiral Craigmont Dorrity.

"This is Gideon, S7A3N0D75#Marburg per PDD-3071. I trust that this is a secure line."

"Yes, Sir," Adm. Dorrity responded.

Sybil then chose to use her normal speaking voice. It would be very soon when the admiral learned her identity, one of the most strictly guarded secrets in the country.

"I have to admit that I am a bit taken aback to hear a woman's voice. And, I beg your pardon, Ma'am; but I recognize it. Wolf News, right?"

"Right. How are plans going for Adm. Jennings to get on board the *Eisenhower*?"

"Swimmingly. The man is like all of my DCNOs. He lives, breathes, and sleeps his ambition to succeed me. It is obvious that he sees the opportunity being offered him as a major step up towards that goal."

"And everyone is cooperating to take advantage of his venality, it seems."

"Yes, Ma'am. They have done a best sailor's effort to contain their hatred and disdain for the traitor. He should be in his stateroom on the ship right now."

"At sea?"

"Yes. He was helicoptered to the ship this morning."

"While we were rounding up the NCIS agent. Incidentally, I'm not sure you heard, but we collected a trunkful of evidence. It will take weeks to sort through it all, but the earliest superficial look indicated a ton of contact with al Qaeda in Saudi Arabia and the corpse of his girl-friend. SecNav has been informed."

"Nice guy—our Special Agent Jacobsen; but now that we have control over him, we can concentrate on my DCNO, may his soul rot in hell. Let's wait two days before we fly you out to the ship. I know you've gone over the plan ad nauseam with DCIA-CT Coxworthy, SecNav Terwilliger, and Director Baxter from the NCIS. I might add that Baxter and Terwilliger have made great progress in closing leaks at NCIS. Are you comfortable with your part in the upcoming theatrical production aboard ship?"

"I am. Hopefully, it won't be all that dramatic."

"Let's hope. Thanks for the update."

Sybil had two and a half days before she had to be at Quantico to catch her marine helicopter flight out to the *Eisenhower*. She did not have to make much of any preparation for her role—she was on the program agenda to tell about slow viruses, including Marburg and HIV disease. She boned up on Kuru, the weird disease contracted by islanders who practiced ritual cannibalization by eating the brains of their departed loved ones—most of whom had died of Kuru themselves. It was pretty grisly but should be entertaining. She knew exactly what she had to do with the traitorous vice-admiral.

She took half a day to show Cerisse around the Washington zoo, and on a tour of the congressional side of the capitol building—pre-arranged through their congresswoman. Charles was in Europe for his company. At noon, she told Cerisse that she had to get back to work and that Cerisse had to get back to school; so, she would not get a demerit.

The Virginia countryside was lush green and beautiful. The country roads were narrow and winding but very well kept. She saw the roof and chimneys of the mansion in the distance and almost missed the obscure entry road into the estate. She rounded a curve and had to stop fairly abruptly for a heavy electronic steel gate.

Two camouflage uniformed guards holding MP-5s and frowns stepped up to the front doors of her Mercedes and signaled for her to lower the windows.

"What is your business here, Ma'am?"

"I'm Gideon. I'm expected."

"I'll check."

He opened a day planner and studied it briefly.

"Please give me your clearance code."

"S7A3N0D75#Marburg, PDD-3071."

"Thank you, Ma'am. Please stay on the main paved road. Do you know the way?"

"Yes, I do, thank you."

Mac was waiting at the front door. He looked at her with complete amazement.

"You're Gideon?!" he said.

"I am. No one else needs to know that, of course."

"Sure. Incredible. I expected some grey haired old gnome—and male at that."

"Let's get to work. Lead on, MacDuff."

Mac led her into the main part of the first floor of the house, through a door to the basement which looked like anyone else's cluttered storage space.

"Can you see it?" he asked.

"The next entryway? No, I can't."

"I'll pass on the compliment to the construction guys. It's right here."

He twisted a mop handle sitting in a large wheeled bucket. On the opposite side of the room, behind Sybil, a panel that looked for all the world like a stack of ¾" plywood panels, rotated outward to reveal a grey concrete hallway with bare light bulbs at intervals to make it possible to navigate through it. Along each side of the tunnel-like passage there were cells. All but one had a black curtain drawn over the barred door. That cell with no curtain was empty except for some very utilitarian furniture and microphones. One wall held a large mirror. On the other side of that cell, there was a room with a door. Mac led Sybil to a seat in front of the two-way mirror.

"I'll get the prisoner," he said.

The door to the cell opened, and Mac led in a very subdued and much chastened young man.

"Sit," Mac said and pointed at the steel chair facing the mirror.

Mark M. Sharron, aka Muntisir Muhammad Shamon sat down wearily. He looked hungry, tired, and frightened.

Sybil began to speak using her voice distortion equipment to make her sound like Elvis Pressley.

"Muntisir, do you know why you are here?"

"I think so."

"Why?"

"Well, I, uh, I falsified my application documents."

"That's a good start. You were asked a hard question, and you told the truth. Now relax, and do the same for a few more questions. If that goes well, we may be able to make it so your stay here; and, indeed, the rest of your life, does not have to be so hard. Do you understand?"

"I am so glad to hear a human voice. I thought I would go nuts sitting in the dark with nothing to do. Even if you are going to torture me, it will be better than that isolation."

Sybil thought, "*And that is exactly what the past two days were supposed to accomplish.*"

Out loud she said, "First question: you entered the United States on a Pakistani passport in 1998 and sometime thereafter became Mark M. Sharron. You have relatives in the mountainous region of North Waziristan and South Waziristan with long-standing ties to the Taliban and who are known to have harbored Usama bin Laden during his long effort to escape U.S. justice. Are you still in contact with them?"

"No. I escaped when a Pakistan army raid killed my parents in the Tochi Pass where we lived. My uncles and cousins stayed on to fight, but I saw that it was a chance to get out of the homicidal/suicidal culture of the tribes there. I escaped to Afghanistan and finally worked for the CIA as a guide and interpreter near Kabul. I became a marked man by the Taliban; so, the Company arranged for me to go to America and to get a green card. I have never contacted my family. That would be nothing less than suicide."

"Second question: how did you get the American name?"

"CIA made it happen. They also gave me a job. I haven't had a bit of trouble until you—whoever you are—arrested me."

"We'll check you out, Muntisir. I want to believe you. It will take time. If you are lying to me, you will condemn your mother for bringing you into the world. If you are telling the truth, we will need to contain you; so, you can't reveal anything you know about us or about what has gone on here. Then, you can have a CIA analyst job back someplace in the Middle-East where your language skills and knowledge of the Taliban and al Qaeda can be put to full use. Our FBI will process you through the witness protection program, even get you plastic surgery; so, you can have a new identity. You will never reveal CIA secrets. If you do, I will be there. They call me "Darkness" for a reason. I will come for you with darkness."

"Will you kill me even if I've told the truth?"

"No. You will take a lie detector test this afternoon, and it will be the most thorough of your career. It should take about two weeks to check out your story. I'm afraid you will have to stay here for that time, but we can get you a bit better accommodations. After that, you will have a two year stay in a very secure but also very comfortable place, if you keep your nose clean."

She tapped on the mirror, and Mac left the cell and entered Sybil's observation room.

"Mac, please get him a reasonable cell and some books. Feed him some decent food starting now before the polygraph. If there is no indication of deception or disambiguation on his part, send him to Fort Meade and let them know he needs to stay there for two full years. Inform the FBI; so, they can get going on WITSEC [The United States Federal Witness Protection Program]. I think he is what he says he is, but it's like the old ranchers I used to know in California used to say, 'trust everyone, but brand your cattle'."

"Will do. Are you ready for the next one?"

"Yes. Bring her in."

Gwendolyn Nielson took her seat in the brightly lit and uninviting cell facing the two-way mirror.

"Hello," Sybil said, this time speaking in a Winston Churchill voice thanks to her handy-dandy portable voice distortion gadget.

"Hello, Sir."

"Okay if I call you Gwendolyn?" Sybil asked, hoping to calm the distraught and agitated subject down."

"Yes, Sir."

"Do you know why you're here?"

"I guess so. I got into trouble because I am a gambling addict, and that got worse when I ruined myself with heroin.

It is a big no-no with the Company; I know that; but I thought I would just get fired or have to go to jail or something—not this. I'm terrified."

"Sounds like the truth, and I think you have good reason to be. Tell me, whom do you fear the most—the Delissiano family, or your CIA superiors and security officers?"

"I'm not sure. It has been bad here, but the loan sharks did awful things to me."

She started to cry at the memory.

"What things?"

"Beat me up…hurt me down there."

"Raped you, right?"

"Yes."

"Do you want to be back out on the streets where the Delissiano's can find you?"

"No, but what choice do I have? Prison? be killed by the CIA?"

"Did you ever share the Company's secrets with anyone else? Did the Delissianos offer to forgive your debts in return for giving them information that they could sell to terrorists?"

"Oh, no, Sir. I would rather die first. I love my country. I love my job. I am absolutely loyal. Don't kill me."

"I have another option for you. It may be the toughest of all. Here's the offer: you go into WITSEC. Do you know what that is?"

"Yes, Sir."

"You will move to another city under a new identity where you will kick the heroin and gambling habits. The Company will pay for that, but you cannot even switch over to methadone. You will be drug free, and you will never bet on another thing the rest of your life, not even a shooting craps on the sidewalk or covering bets. Failure is not an option; either you are drug free or you are on your own. Then, the things that go bump in the night will find you."

"I will try my very, very best. It would be like getting a new life."

"Ummhmmh. But there's a catch. First, you have to pass a polygraph test and have one every few months when I ask you to. Second, you will attend meetings. Do you drink as well as shoot up heroin?"

"Just heroin."

"If you are clean and sober for a year, you will come to work as my personal analyst. I will arrange that with the Company. If I get you out of this mess, I will own you. You will be able to have a pretty normal life, if working for the CIA can ever be considered normal. But, you will do what I ask, when I ask. You will drop everything to do my bidding when I do ask. You will find that my requests will be reasonable and usually as legal as anything else you might do for the Company. I want you sober. I prefer that you get married, have kids, become president of the PTA and be an exemplary soccer mom. I will provide some insurance that you can have a normal life. You let me deal with the dealers, okay?"

"I will do every possible thing to live up to make you proud of me. I am smart, and I can be a great help if you just get me back to the living."

"You will have a polygraph test this afternoon. Pass it—no deception. After that, you will go to a safe and comfortable place while the FBI sets you up in WITSEC. Other than the U.S. Marshalls who will keep you safe, only I will know who or where you are."

Mac took Gwendolyn out of the cell. When he came back to the room behind the mirror, he gave Sybil an exaggeratedly quizzical look.

"I suppose it's the same drill?"

"Yes. I want to be kept informed about every development with her.

"Okay. P.S., I thought the way you handled those innocents was great. I hope you go a long way in the Company. We need a thinker like you."

Chapter Ten

"Thanks. But don't give me too much credit. Let's see how it goes with NCIS Special Agent Myron Jacobsen."

Jacobsen was sullen. He had to be shoved onto the chair facing the mirror, and he gave the mirror the finger. It had been a powerful let-down to be forced to tap three times when he decided to become unruly with a guard—three CIA men, including Mac, all of whom bested the NCIS agent who was very much used to putting down the criminals and scaring them straight. He was known to be a remarkably skilled martial artist.

"Myron, it's probably best that you settle down. I'm busy, and I am going to make some proposals you should pay attention to," Sybil said through her voice distortion machine.

She thought this was her favorite of all of the available distortion voices—Betty Boop.

"Lady, you got a silly voice. Anyone ever tell you that? And I am Special Agent Jacobsen to you."

"Myron, my boy. It is probably going to be a shock to you, but you don't get to make demands anymore. You are going to spend the rest of your life in a four by six foot cell, alone 23 hours a day with two lousy high-carb meals in 24 hours. You will have 15 minutes a week—always at eleven o'clock at night—to exercise if you have been a good boy. That is the best case scenario. The other choice is to spend the rest of your life in the cold and in the dark. The same prison you're headed to can manage both ways. What we are going to determine in the next ten or fifteen minutes is which scenario you are going to endure. If it is the dark choice, the only question will be how long will your sanity last?

"You may remember another couple of traitors—Robert Philip Hansson and John Anthony Walker Jr.?"

"Yeah, I remember. How long is this stupid history lesson gonna last, cupie doll?"

"Just long enough to make my point, Myron. I'll let you in on their current lives. Hansson is Federal Bureau of Prisons prisoner #48551-083. He is serving his sentence at the ADX Florence, a federal supermax prison in Florence, Colorado— the meanest prison in America. He is in solitary confinement in a dark windowless cell 23 hours a day. No one is allowed to talk to him. He gets no visitors—ever. His food is served in a ground up ball—two meals a day. The temperature in his cell is never above fifty degrees. He walks outside whether he wants to or not. Florence, Colorado gets real cold in the winter—sometimes below zero. He goes out anyway. He walks around in a concrete silo sort of tower designed to prevent him seeing the sky. He has not seen the sun or the sky since July, 2001.

"It is a little different for Walker even though his espionage crimes may have been even worse. The reason for the difference is that he turned state's evidence against all of his co-conspirators, even his family. He has been in prison for 30 years and will get out on parole in 2015. Prison life has not been so bad for friend, Walker. He is incarcerated in Butner Federal Correctional Complex—the low security section—in Butner, North Carolina. It's warm there in North Carolina. He gets to walk outside pretty much as often as he wants during the day. He gets three fairly good meals a day, gets good medical care, has regular visitors—even with a girlfriend—and is a member of reading, chess, and ping-pong clubs. He attends movies, watches TV, and gets to go to lectures once a month. The difference between the two traitors; Walker ratted everybody out.

"Choose now, Myron. When you go back to your cell, you can prepare for a life of solitude in the dark with nothing to do, or you can go to a country club cell, comparatively speaking. If you choose the "country club," you will start today to list every person who helped you in the slightest way, who got money from your terrorist friends, and where is the rest of your money? We know about the $650,000, and we know there's more. Who were your terrorist contacts? And you will tell us everything there is to know about the traitorous activities of Vice-Admiral Duncan Lloyd Jennings, DCNO—the N2/N6 and the DNI. You will not leave out a single detail, and you will not lie. It may take weeks, but you will do your work. Lie or cheat us in the least degree, and the deal is off—darkness, solitude, and mind-destroying boredom for the rest of your life.

"Choose now, Myron, my boy. I will leave the room in one minute."

When Betty Boop told him about Adm. Jennings, the bottom dropped out of his hopes. Jennings was going to go down and was certainly not going to bail him out. Myron figured that he had to get the deal first. He never did believe in the booshwa about "honor among thieves."

"Okay, I'll rat. You gotta protect me, and I get a signed contract from SecNav."

"But, of course, Myron. That would only be fair. Do your job. Don't fail me. I am not nice, and I can make your life a lot less nice that you have every imagined in your nightmares."

One of the guards knocked on the door of room with the two-way mirror and delivered an interoffice message in a TOP SECRET government manila envelope. It was marked "URGENT" and "EYES-ONLY, GIDEON."

There was a single sheet of paper in the envelope.

From: Agent Estroy, document section OHB

To: Code Name Gideon

Urgent

Re: Evidence files obtained during arrest of Special NCIS Agent Myron Jacobsen

Message:

Information incomplete. Two e-mail documents contain a list of four individuals, dated yesterday:

-Special Agent CIA Alfred Knox Whitehead, presently in London, location—separate communication

-Special Agent CIA Clarisse Mountford, presently in Kabul, location uncertain

-Special Agent CIA Sybil Norcroft, M.D., F.A.C.S., presently in New York, location Wolf News Headquarters. Travels extensively.

-Special Agent CIA Donald Peterson, whereabouts unknown as of this message. Presumed dead.

-Action-locate and terminate as per order 6 from NI One and Agency Chiefs.

Sybil was shocked at the reality of seeing her name on an official hit list. She knew that her enemies were determined and resourceful—they had been successful four times in the last year—but she was very much taken aback to realize that the NCIS clandestine espionage unit was able to find her and the other agents despite such elaborate efforts to preserve secrecy and security. She cleared her head and walked into the darkened hall to catch Mac as soon as he returned from moving Myron Jacobsen to the cell where he was to begin writing his confession. "Urgent" was not nearly a strong enough word for the situation.

"Mac, Jacobsen got the names of three of the remaining ultra top-secret deep cover agents and me. The plans are to assassinate all of us, and I presume that the time frame is very short. Take a look at this message from Langley."

Mac perused the message in two seconds.

"I'll get the message out to the response teams of both the CIA and the FBI ASAP. They will get protection details to all of the agents including you. Sybil, my orders are to protect you as first priority. You are to wait here until your security detail can mount up. The seventh floor will alert the other agents on the list to go to ground if that is even possible. From this point on, we will not trust anyone except the response teams that show up here. You with me, boss?"

It was clear that Mac was the boss in this situation, and Sybil nodded her understanding and agreement.

"My family needs protection. Now!" she said.

"I'm on it. Let's head back to the OHB, and I'll have the security detail fetch your family there."

"My daughter and a neighbor lady who is staying with her are the only ones in my home. My husband is staying in the Hotel de Crillon in Paris. He should be in bed about now."

"We'll protect them, Sybil. You need to worry about yourself. Let's go get suited up."

Mac and Sybil put on Kevlar vests with ceramic bullet proof plates and Kevlar thigh and shoulder pads and helmets. They found Sam Browne belts with Colt 1911 .45 hand guns, lightweight MAC-10s, combat k-bar knives, flares, handcuffs, flashlights, and flash-bang grenades. The twenty-two pound weight around her waist was going to be a test for Sybil. Mac picked out an AR-15 for himself and a combat shotgun for Sybil to carry. He placed four full boxes of ammunition magazines on a dolly which they wheeled out to the front entrance to await in readiness for the cavalry to arrive.

"Do you think Adm. Jennings got Jacobsen's message, Mac? That would let him make plans for escape and would queer our plans at sea. Besides, it frosts me that this could mean that that murdering weasel, Jacobsen, could get the last laugh after all."

"I'm pretty sure Jennings has been sequestered communications-wise since before Jacobsen's message went out. I think we're safe there, but it's a good thought. I'll get a message out to the CNO's office and to the DCIA. The nice people asleep in their beds tonight are going to be unaware that a war is taking place, I think."

"I hope," Sybil added.

Three fully armored black Humvees arrived while Mac was finishing his communica-tions.

Chapter Eleven

It was midnight. The HMMWV [High Mobility Multipurpose Wheeled Vehicle] convoy raced through the nearly empty streets of Loudoun County with lights and sirens blazing and blaring. The civilian population was, for the most part, tucked in their beds; and law enforcement was aware of the convoy's critical mission and need to exceed the speed limits. They provided additional security cover. Traffic began to pick up some when they turned right onto South King Street (U.S.-15 Branch) and increased still more as they turned onto the Leesburg Bypass for half a mile. When they turned to the right on the Dulles Greenway East, they began to run into late night airport traffic headed into IAD [Dulles International Airport]. Although the risks of attack were expected to increase the slower they went, Sybil began to relax. The speeding and risk of an accident seemed more imminent and in the present than a theoretical attack.

The convoy was able accelerate after they turned onto the VA-123 ramp towards McLean. They turned almost immediately onto Waverly Way, and again immediately turned right onto Chain Bridge Road. As the lead Humvee cleared the off ramp, a camouflage painted troop truck roared off from a hiding place on the road's gravel margin and plowed through the Humvee putting it and its security guard occupants completely out of commission.

Sybil and Mac were in the back seat of the second unit in the convoy.

Mac shouted to the driver, "Get around the mess. Put the pedal to the metal." To Sybil and the other CIA security guards, he snapped, "Lock and load. We're in for a fight. One of you call the OHB switchboard and have them send the cavalry. Keep your heads down."

The driver was a professional military defensive driving instructor. The Humvee has a wide, low base and held to the road by some miracle as the large heavy vehicle lurched and bounced—sometimes on only two wheels—and sometimes on the road and sometimes off in the barrow pit. And somehow, the vehicle avoided rolling over. Somewhere along the way, they ran over something that produced a sickening thud highly suggestive that they had hit a body.

A troop truck and two large armored Suburbans raced after Sybil and Macs' Humvee. Now automatic rifle fire was zinging bullets off the bullet proof skin of the powerful vehicle and presumably into the tires which were supposedly bullet proof.

Looking out the back window, Max shouted, "Incoming—rocket!!" immediately before a deafening crash and a ball of flame enveloped the Hummer sending it into a figure-of-eight double circle. Both rear wheels were now missing, and the security conveyance ground a stream of sparks from the asphalt and stopped abruptly. Fire was licking at the engine compartment.

"Fire. Everybody out. Commence firing as soon as you hit the ground," Mac yelled and threw himself out onto the gravel.

He rolled quickly to a kneeling position and began firing blindly at twelve enemy combatants who were jumping out of the back of the truck. Sybil and her two guards followed Mac's lead and rolled out guns blazing. One of the guards was killed by a head wound before he could assume an effective shooting stance. Sybil was hit twice in the ceramic plates of her Kevlar vest and was knocked down as if some giant had punched her. The other guard threw himself protectively over her as she lay trying to find some breath.

The fighting was the equivalent of a military "mad-minute" with both sides pouring in their ammunition as fast as their weapons could operate. The third Humvee in the caravan plowed into the side of the enemy troop truck causing it to lurch out of control, skid, and to turn on its side. The security guards were shaken but not really hurt. They jumped out and ran to the truck killing everyone in it. The driver put the Humvee into reverse and blew a sand storm of gravel getting back onto the asphalt. His passengers jumped back into the Humvee and reloaded as they rushed towards the fiery fire fight half a mile further on. Someone launched a second LAWs rocket and caused a second huge explosion and fire.

"Get off me, I'm okay," Sybil said—more accurately coughed out—to the guard whose body was protecting her.

She was nearly deaf from the explosion and a little bewildered. She could see the bullets striking the burning Humvee better than she could hear them. The night and the fight had a surreal quality. She slapped herself to bring her mind back into focus.

Mac had been hurled well off into the roadside bushes by the last salvo from the still relatively intact enemy unit. His bell had been rung, and he could not get it together enough to resume fighting for several minutes.

Sybil and her guard rolled frantically to get away from the burning security vehicle and into the relative security and obscurity of the heavy brush beyond the margin of the road. He was grazed on his left arm below his Kevlar shoulder pad. Sybil had a very sore chest but figured that she was still viable and functional. For a minute, she lay in quiet obscurity. Evidently the brilliance of the explosion hid the rolling escape of her and the guard. She waited until she had a reasonably clear shot then began firing rounds at the enemies' heads. In the confusion, four of them died from her shots, and two were killed by their own men as collateral damage.

The third Humvee roared lights off up behind the killers' truck and stopped suddenly. The—as yet, unscathed—CIA security guards leaped out and rolled over the ground to a kneeling shooter's stance and commenced firing a deadly accurate fusillade. Three more enemy combatants dropped. Sybil killed a fourth one of those remaining in combat. Her guard stood up in a gesture of exceptional bravery or incredible foolhardiness and opened up with withering automatic rifle fire catching the killers in a deadly pincer.

From Langley, four fast cars roared in and surrounded the remaining three killers, one of whom was badly wounded.

"Cease fire," Sybil yelled. "Take them alive. We need to interrogate them."

Six men from the ring of cars that came from Langley and another six from the Humvee raced towards the remaining two killers still standing. The mercenary killers saw no point in heroism—theirs was a lost cause, one which they did not believe in; it was just the money. They threw down their weapons and dropped prone to the ground with their hands on the back of their heads, fingers interlocked. The twelve security agents quickly placed handcuffs and leg irons on the mercs and loaded them aboard the Humvee.

Sybil met Mac—who had regained the use of his thinker—and together they gathered with the security agents.

Sybil said, "Take them to the seventh floor interrogation holding cells and place them on full security and suicide watch. Special Agent Young, here, will carry on the interrogation. Please do not talk to them until he can get as much information as possible."

The lead security agent asked, "You Gideon, Ma'am?"

"Yes."

"We was expecting a man. You're quite a surprise and a terrific shot."

He gave her a high-five.

"You obeyed all the rules of a gun fight tonight, Ma'am: the most important rule in a gunfight is—always win. There is no such thing as a fair fight. Always win—cheat if necessary. If you're not shooting, you should be loading. If you're not loading, you should be moving. If you're not moving, you're dead."

"I'll try and remember all that," Sybil said with a smile.

Max made a call.

"Your daughter and her baby sitter are safe and sound in their beds in the OHB visitors' quarters. Apparently Cerisse has found the whole evening very stimulating…says she wants to be a spy."

Sybil took the phone, "Cerisse?"

"Yes, Mama."

"You are up past your bedtime, sweetheart. It's three o'clock in the morning. You okay?"

"I am. It's been fun, but I kind of worried about you."

"I'm fine. I had a busy night. Sorry I couldn't get home to tuck you in tonight. I still have a couple or three more days of work, then we'll have another car trip. How does that sound?"

"Great. Can't wait. Night, Mama."

"Night, Cerisse. Sleep tight and don't let the bedbugs bite."

Next Sybil made three calls in rapid succession. The first was to the president to inform him about the attack and to report that one of the mercs admitted that he could give details of the assassination of Special Agent CIA Donald Peterson and a great deal of more information in return for immunity. President Willets expressed his relief that she was all right and ordered her to let the potential informant stew for a while before granting immunity.

"Things are peaceful now Mr. President. I will get to the ship tomorrow; and hopefully, we'll finish this."

"Thomas Jefferson put it best, Sybil: 'Peace is that brief glorious moment in history, when everybody stands around reloading'."

Sybil laughed, "I think he got that right."

The second call was to Charles Daniels, her husband, in the Hotel de Crillon in Paris. He asked her how things were going; she told him a little fib, "Real busy, but okay, I guess."

The third call was on behalf of Gwendolyn Nielson.

Chapter Twelve

It was 0415. Rodrigo Delissiano received a weird call on his very private cell phone.

"Who's this? How'd youse get this number? Better have a real good answer or youse're toast."

"Never mind," the Humphrey Bogart voice answered on a burner phone, "it doesn't matter who I am, but it is worth your life to do what I say."

"You threatenin' me—the don here in D.C.?"

"I am. You are a CI [Confidential Informant] for the FBI. I have recordings of your meetings where you sell out two *capo bastones*, one *consigliere*, and half a dozen *caporegimes* over the last five years—all from other families, and all unauthorized by the commission. I can give the tape and a description to the other six bosses, or I can ask a favor from you."

"Whadda youse want?" Rodrigo answered in his guttural voice that sounded that he had just finished a session of gargling gravel.

"A favor, like I said. This is it: your Soriano set has a loan sharking client whom I don't want to be bothered any more.

Her name is Gwendolyn Nielson. A couple of the Sorianos got her addicted to gambling and heroin, beat her up, threatened her, and raped her. Their names are Miguel Soriano, Guido Musalla, and Antonio "Big Boy" Catallini. The first thing is that you forget her debts. The second thing is you forget all about her, forever. The third thing is that you see to it that the capo, Guillermo Soriano, and his three thugs take a long boat ride on rough seas."

"Youse don' ask much, do youse?"

"Not that much considering what I have on you. You have forty-six million dollars in a Cayman Island bank account. All I have to do is to press a 'send' button on my computer, and it's mine. Oh, in case you think I'm bluffing, your account number is 23J-892Y-4*1209. Your password is not all that clever. You can do better than RD10.30.67—your birthday?—really!?"

"Okay, okay. After that youse'll lay off, right?"

"I will. But if you fail in any part of our deal, you will read about your deal with the feds in the newspaper and see it in a very clear video on all the news networks. I will personally let your loyal friends—the other dons—know in advance of the public media release. *Capiche*? Roddy, baby doll?"

That last reference stung and frightened the crime boss the most. It was the term of endearment that his long-time mistress used.

"I *capiche*," Rodrigo said sourly.

Sybil hung up.

The adrenaline rush wore off, and Sybil slept in the marine helicopter on the way out to sea to get aboard the *Eisenhower*. She had stuffed some dungarees and tee shirts, underwear and socks, a couple of dressy casual outfits, an evening gown and some jewelry, a combat knife and her—now overly familiar—Glock .30. She was too sleepy to worry about what she might have left behind.

The marine helicopter landed on one of the helipads on the great ship's deck. The USS *Dwight D. Eisenhower* was commissioned as the second of ten nuclear-powered Nimitz-class aircraft carriers—the backbone of the United States navy. The carrier is the flagship of CVN-69 [Cruiser Vessel-Nuclear propulsion] battle group, one of the groups that can conduct World War III by itself. The sea was calm—for which Sybil was thankful—and allowed for a bright clear view of the cobalt blue ocean from horizon to horizon. From a distance the ship looked tiny; and—-like every novice—Sybil could not imagine that the helicopter could land on such a spec.

When the marine helicopter was just above the landing deck, Sybil became duly impressed with the immensity of the majestic carrier. Like its seven sisters, the "mighty *Ike*" is a self-sustained floating airport that is sovereign U.S. territory and is defended as such. When deployed at sea, it is capable of operating with its own ZIP code, post office, hospital, dental clinic, barbershops, athletic facilities, and chapels. More than 18,000 meals are prepared daily and each of the crew has e-mail access. The one exception to that e-mail access was the most senior ranking officer, Vice-Admiral Duncan Lloyd Jennings, whose electronic transmissions were all rerouted to the ship's intelligence office and stored without being sent further on. His incoming e-mails were screened and sanitized before sending them on to him.

When her helicopter landed, the carrier's captain—Rear Admiral George C. Titcomb—came down from the "island"—the superstructure containing the bridg—to welcome their celebrity guest aboard. The highest ranking officer aboard came down from his VIP stateroom suite—2-2-3 L—as well. Both of their aides and Master Chief Dirk Kenyon, the ship's senior enlisted man—and head of the Quarterdeck detail—were present when Sybil alighted from the helicopter.

She was piped aboard and saluted by all hands present. She faced the deck flag and placed her right hand over her heart. Master Chief Kenyon gave the formal welcome.

"Welcome aboard Dr. Norcroft. We have looked forward to your coming. We hope you will enjoy fair winds and a following sea while you are aboard. Here is the administrative information you will need while on the "Mighty *Ike*."

"Thank you, Master Chief," she said.

Adm. Titcomb greeted her next, "May I add my welcome, Dr. Norcroft. If there is anything that you need from the bridge, please let us know."

"Thank you, Sir. That is most generous. About all I might ask for is not to get seasick and to have a guide dog to keep me from getting lost."

Sybil and the men laughed.

Vice-Adm. Jennings saluted her and said, "I echo the welcome. I will be having a small introductory party in your honor in my suite at 8 bells at the start of the last dog watch. I wish you all the best and hope you can join us."

"You could not keep me away, Sir. Thanks."

Sybil was shown to her quarters and learned what the number system meant. She was assigned to 3-7-3 L, the deck level below the vice-admiral's stateroom suite. She made both a physical and a mental note to remind her and to keep her from getting hopelessly lost in the labyrinth of the floating city. A Nimitz-class carrier has 18 levels, including eight above the ship's enormous hangar bay and ten decks below. Her living quarters were three levels down from the top, near the front, in the seventh compartment outboard of the centerline to port, and on the starboard side. "L" stands for "Living quarters." It was six bells of the afternoon watch [1500 hrs], and Sybil could not keep her eyes open. She set her iPhone alarm for five bells of the last dog watch [1830 hrs] and slept the sleep of the dead.

She was awakened twenty minutes early by a soft knock on her door. She picked up her Glock and chambered a round.

"Who is it?"

"A friend of Gideon's."

"Who is Gideon?"

"I don't know, but I have a message. It involves criminal activity on and off the "*Ike*" and also one of the deputy CNOs. Please don't keep me out here in the hallway."

The honest answer persuaded Sybil. She let the man in but kept her Glock leveled at his chest.

"Speak," she said.

"On board ship here, I am Lieutenant Commander Russell Philips, the supervising officer of the ship's stores. That puts me into an advantageous position to learn about almost everything that enters of leaves the ship. I have information to send out which is too secret to send by any system other than word of mouth. How do I know that you have the clearance?"

"I have an Ultra TS/SCI [Above Top Secret] clearance rating with SSBI [Single Scope Background Investigation] as is covered in PDD-3071. You may contact the president directly using your TS code then tell him you need information to verify Gideon. Describe what I look like and where I am. That is probably the most serious secret in the U.S. today. Come back when you have verified it, and we can talk."

"I'll be back in 20 or 30."

It was 40, but who was keeping track?

"So," Sybil said, this time keeping her Glock safely on the lamp table and not pointing it at Philips.

"You're good, Dr. Norcroft. Your name and information was magic. I am directed by the president and the DCIA-CT to give you any information and any assistance you may need."

"First off, I need something written or encoded that I can send to the DCIA, DCIA-CT and a copy that has a lot of misinformation to use for my mission in chief on board the "*Ike*."

"We need to meet away from the residences. I should not be here, and it would be very awkward to be seen anywhere near your room."

"You have already been seen. My guards are aware of you and will protect both of us."

"Any ideas about where we could meet and make the information transfer. I have a few, but I am so skittish that I don't know if I am even rational anymore. What I know is enough to get me killed, and there are sailors here looking for me."

"I think I am going to catch a case of seasickness," Sybil said, "I will be in sick-bay within the hour. My guards will be there as well because I am going to have to persuade the Chief Pharmacist's Mate to cooperate. If I can't, we will have to put him in seclusion and close the dispensary. I guess I jumped to a conclusion. I hope against hope that the pharmacist's mate is not part of your drug smuggling suspects."

"No, he's clean. He is even working with me. He's a good guy and once convinced that our mission is honorable and necessary for national security, he will be a great help."

"That's a definite plus. I'll meet you there in fifteen minutes or so. For one thing, I have to figure out how to get to the dispensary."

She found out without difficulty. Charles was always mildly amazed at his wife's ability in orienteering both in the wild and in cities. He complained of being dependent on Sybil.

She signed in with the third class pharmacist's mate and waited until she was called back to see the nurse. Philips slipped into the examination room and informed the nurse that the new patient needed to see the Chief. It seemed slightly odd, but the nurse was too busy to argue and fetched her superior.

Philips introduced Sybil.

Sybil said, "Chief, we have a serious issue to discuss and need your help. May I ask what your security clearance is?"

The chief looked at Philips for assurance. Philips nodded.

"Secret," the chief answered Sybil.

"That will have to do. I have a very serious mission—truly one of national security level importance. I want you to check me out now and then to do several things I ask—some of them may well seem not to be kosher, but believe me they are legal and need to be done."

The President of the United States received his second personal call from the carrier *Dwight D. Eisenhower* that evening. Once again, he convinced the enlisted man of Sybil's bona fides.

"I'm in," Chief Drahher said.

"This is what I need," Sybil said, "chloroform, injectable phenobarb, a body bag, and an IV of D$_5$NS. Mr. Philips, please get some handcuffs from the brig, duct tape from ship's stores, and a ten-foot length of rope. Any ideas what we can use to cover a man who is going to depart the ship AWOL?"

"Cripes, this is beginning to sound creepy," Philips said, "when do you need that stuff?"

"About eight tonight. I can't have any of it on my person. I am going to a party in the vice-admiral's stateroom suite. I'll step out at an appropriate moment, and you can hand over the goods to my guards who will be part of this."

Are the guards those two giants in the waiting room?" Chief Drahher asked.

Sybil nodded.

"I have to go and fix my face, but first I am going to tell you what's up. Sit down. I think you will need to be seated when I explain all of this."

Both LCDR Philips and Chief Drahher went a little white when the name of the DCNO, Vice-Admiral Duncan Lloyd Jennings, entered the conversation. They might have fainted when she unfolded her audacious plan.

The party was a grand affair. There is nothing more attractive than a naval officer in full dress whites, sword, gold buttons, gold braid, and scrambled eggs on the brim of his hat to conjure images of the glory of war and the excitement of the sea. The room was full of officers who conjured up images of power and strength for Sybil. On the other hand, Sybil quickly became the center of attention—lithe, beautiful, voluptuous in a medium deep décolletage, and a blood red evening gown. She had jewels, a winning smile, and star power which had preceded her because of her Wolf News fame.

There was considerable heavy drinking going on around the room, and the Filipino ship's stewards were kept busy. Like all other sailors, they were on 24/7 watch, and looked rather tired to her.

When she mentioned that opinion to the XO of the ship, he laughed and said, "It's all too true and all too necessary. Since time immemorial idle sailors have gotten into trouble and played havoc with good ship's order. From the old British war ships, the philosophy was 'Six days shalt thou labor and do all that thou art able. The sixth is to cork the deck and holystone the cable."

Sybil laughed appreciatively and genuinely. She liked the salty quality of the veterans of the sea. She like their weathered brown faces and ramrod straight bodies. She did not mind the gentlemanly flirting, and was rather flattered.

She had been enjoying the party for over forty-five minutes before the host, the ranking officer on board the *Dwight D. Eisenhower,* Vice-Admiral Duncan Lloyd Jennings, himself, found his way over to her. He was tall, patrician, handsome, and affable. He had a winning smile with large, even, white teeth. His most striking feature was his shock of wavy pure white hair which had obviously been perfectly coiffed by a professional. For all his authority and power, he seemed to take a genuine interest in all of his guests, including those whom he outranked by multiple steps.

"Dr. Norcroft. It is nice to see you again. I hope you have been enjoying the day. The sea is nice and calm; the sky and the ocean are clear and deep blue; and there is no wind. Get out and get a tan. I'll look forward to hearing your talk tomorrow night. Have fun at the party," he said as he artfully slipped away to meet-and-greet the next guest.

She agreed with him; she would certainly see him again. As the evening drew to a close, Sybil watched the guests leave. They showed themselves out, and neither the admiral nor his servants seemed to man the door. That worked well for her plan. She found a door wedge left by the cleaning crew earlier in the day; and when no one was paying attention, she bent down by the door to adjust the strap on her shoe and pressed the door wedge under the bottom of the door so that it remained open a couple of inches.

At eleven-thirty, the last few stragglers—most of them two sheets to the wind from fine wine and champagne—made their way to the door. Sybil took cover in the bathroom; so, she could be the last to leave. She had concocted a plausible excuse.

When she was reasonably sure that only the she and the admiral were left in his quarters, she stepped back into the main bedroom and quietly padded towards the door.

"Ah, Dr. Norcroft," came Jennings's rich baritone voice. "I thought you had left with all the others."

"I would have," she lied, "but I got a touch of seasickness. I'm not much of a sailor, I've learned."

His face was not nearly so affable now.

"Oh, Doctor, do stay for a while. We have so much to talk about."

He was more than a head taller than she was and outweighed her by more than forty pounds. He advanced towards her.

She backed up towards the door.

"What's the hurry, Sybil? We need to have a discussion. It seems we have some mutual friends—one, at least."

"And who is that, sir?" she asked working to keep the fear out of her voice.

"Well...LCDR Russell Philips, for one. I've had my eye on him for several months, or more accurately, some of my people have been keeping track of him. It seems that he has been keeping secrets from me. As you no doubt know, I am the head honcho of the secrets factory for the navy. It is bad form to keep secrets from me."

"What sort of secrets, Admiral?"

"Aren't you the coy one? I think you probably know the answer to that one better than I do. My eyes and ears were on to you today—a little clandestine meeting in your quarters. Maybe a tryst? But I don't think so. He doesn't seem to be your type. I think he's more the unsavory type. A spy, maybe. What do you think?"

She edged closer to the door. She could not be sure that her security men were out there and close enough to get into the admiral's stateroom in time to protect her. She decided on the oldest trick of them all. She started to cry and was proud of herself being able to cry on demand.

"Oh, no. I've made you cry. Why is that?"

"You're frightening me. I don't know what this is about, and it is making me very uncomfortable."

She reached her hand into her small purse and fumbled for a tissue. What she actually did was to pour a portion of liquid from the vial of chloroform onto a square of fine cotton cloth.

"Here, allow me," Adm. Jennings said.

He reached out for her purse. She backed up quickly and was able to insert her right toes into the crack of the door she had created earlier in the evening.

Jennings wrapped his large hand around her slim wrist and worked to pull her back into the room.

"No, no," he said, "I'm afraid you are going to have to share your secrets that came from LCDR Philips. You see, ship's security is at his door as we speak. He is going to complete his tour of duty in the brig. While he is there, he is going to tell me what he has been up to. One of my people suggested that it might have to do with heroin. I'm afraid you're involved as well, and you are going to have to answer for that."

"Could be, Admiral," Sybil said coldly, her hard blue eyes holding his in thrall.

She did not resist as he pulled on her arm ever more strongly. He did not want her to scream and to draw attention to what was going on.

"And I am going to find out right now everything you know."

He jerked her arm and would have pulled it out of the socket had she resisted. But she did not resist. Instead she suddenly lurched forward closing the distance between them to nil. He was surprised, but she was prepared. It was judo—the gentle way—give in to gain the advantage. Her right hand swiped like lightening out of her hand bag and thrust the cloth dripping with chloroform over his mouth and nose. Adm. Jennings was so surprised that he made an outcry, one which no one heard. The inhalation that was part of his intended yell sucked a minor overdose of the powerful anesthetic into his lungs.

Murder showed in his eyes; and, for a moment, he wrenched and twisted her arm. She bent with him and watched as his eyes glazed over and ceased to struggle as did the rest of his body. Sybil's foot in the door flipped it open, and Jennings's hand dropped away from her bruised arm. He crumpled to the ground, all fight gone out of him.

Her guards burst silently through the door.

"Are you okay, Gideon?" the larger of the two asked.

"She seems to have handled things quite well by herself. What is the rest of the plan, boss?"

LCDR Philips—not his real name of course—and Chief Pharmacist's Mate Drahher brought up the rear. Chief Drahher held a needle and syringe and inserted it into the admiral's triceps through his uniform sleeve.

"What was that, Chief?" Sybil asked, beginning to calm down.

"A little phenobarb, Doctor. Enough to keep him asleep for about fourteen hours—enough to get him to a secure place."

"Nice touch," Sybil said and squeezed his shoulder.

"Ah shucks, us humble workers in the dispensary and clinic seldom have any excitement. This will go down as a red letter day for me."

"And, he's going to go down for moving millions of dollars' worth of heroin using the *Eisenhower* and the *Nimitz* as his personal storage and distribution center. In the conduct of his rotten business, there is no telling how many U.S. sailors he compromised. Makes you want to hurt him, don't it?" he asked rhetorically.

"That's not the half of it," Sybil said. "Now we have to finish what we've started. Commander Philips, did you signal the helicopter?"

"On his way down as we speak."

"Chief, did you get through to the captain?"

"I did, but it was unnecessary. The CNO has been in regular contact with him. He knows that unfortunate Adm. Jennings is going to suffer a terrible accident and will see to it that a grand and sorrowful memorial service is held on the ship and that his widow receives the whole host of benefits due her for the loss of her beloved while in the line of duty. I have to tell you that it 'frosted my butt' the captain said, to have to turn a blind eye to everything this man has done."

"I plan to wring every scintilla of information the man possesses before he goes away to spend the rest of his life in solitary semi-darkness. I will see to it that he never sees the sun, never feels the rain, and never has a visitor. In fact, Vice-Admiral Duncan Lloyd Jennings will cease to exist from this day forward, but he will live out a full life as a number with a million days to remember every crime he has committed. We Americans don't like traitors, murderers, or drug lords, and he was all of those. Let's get him out of here before the marine helicopter landing draws attention."

The six of them quickly handcuffed Jennings and put his ankles in shackles. His eyes and mouth were covered with heavy black duct tape—monster tape. Then they wrapped the anesthetized admiral in a camouflage blanket and carried him to the heliport and loaded him onto the aircraft. Philips got on as well, and when the admiral's trussed and covered body was out of sight, two burly marine brig guards duck-walked the two security guards who assisted the admiral in all of his pursuits—legal and illegal—onto the helicopter. With no fanfare, the chopper rose straight up and was out of sight in about a minute.

Chief Drahhan walked Sybil back to her quarters with the faithful guards bringing up the rear, ever watchful for the safety of their national security "treasure" as President Willets had described her to them.

Sybil spent the next two days on board to preserve her cover story. She gave her two speeches and won a thousand or two friends or admirers and even some love-sick boys who sent her flowers and cards.

Chapter Thirteen

Sybil had been away from her work at Wolf News, had ignored her friend, Raza Patel's, entreaties to join him in enough neurosurgical operations to keep up her active membership in the AANS [American Association of Neurological Surgeons], and was receiving nastygrams from her feminist colleagues. But, her main regret and need for repentance was that she had neglected her husband and adopted daughter.

In order of importance, she elected to take a good solid car trip with them, and to worry about the rest of them later. She had collected enough "attaboy points" from her spymasters to keep them off her back for months. They would have to wait as well. She even demurred when she received an invitation to a White House dinner for prominent Americans.

The family flew to Portland, Oregon and rented a Cadillac Escalade ESV. They drove north on I-5 to see Mt. St. Helens and then west on Oregon 30 to the Lewis and Clark National Wildlife Refuge. Cerisse was full of questions about the epic transcontinental journey of the Lewis and Clark expedition and excited to see the western end of that historical trek because she had written a paper for school about it. She told Sybil and Charles that she was "very proud of our forefathers." They hired a guide in Astoria for two days and fished for sturgeon. Cerisse was thrilled to be the only one to catch a fish—a 248 pound sturgeon—which fed the family two meals and a homeless shelter for a month. The guide even convinced Cerisse to help clean the fish and was surprised when the diminutive girl got right into the job and was not the least bit squeamish. She saw the Pacific Ocean for the first time at the point a few miles south of Astoria where the Columbia River ends into the Pacific Ocean. They were all excited with the tour of Fort Clatsop which was the winter encampment for the Corps of Discovery.

Like every other car load of vacationers, the Daniels's left Astoria, the northern most part of the Oregon coast, and headed south to see: Haystack Rock on Cannon Beach, the two Tillamook cheese factories, the Three Capes Scenic Loop, Devil's Punchbowl State Park, and Newport with its Oregon Coast Aquarium and the Hatfield Marine Science Center. Cerisse developed her life's ambition to be a marine biologist there—an obsession that lasted a week when she decided that she wanted to be a neurosurgeon like her mother. During their visit to the reputedly haunted Yaquina Bay Lighthouse, Cerisse regaled her parents with real ghost stories from the Congo. Charles worried that their daughter was reliving the sources of her PTSD, but Sybil convinced him to let her get it all out. It did seem to be cathartic and helpful for the little pygmy girl with such a frightening past.

They left off their rental car at the Hertz lot in the San Francisco International Airport and flew home. Cerisse was excited to get back to see all around San Francisco and the Bay Area. She had a day's—maybe two, days'—worth of fascinating tales to tell her classmates at the Visitation Preparatory School in Georgetown. The experience had one very positive result. Cerisse was able to occupy her own bedroom without having the terrors of the night force her into her parents' bed.

Sybil reported back to Wolf News and taped three health related stories written for her by staff writers. Doug Mason's videos provided the color and background. Her boss, David Kilcannon, vice-president of Wolf News production, was somewhat put off about her past, and now impending, absences from her prominent part in the news and told her of his concerns, the most serious of which was the fall in her own and the channel's ratings. During the past month and a half, Raza Patel over at WWN had regained the lead over her.

"I have to do a very important thing at the request of the president, David. I am pretty sure I can be back in a week or ten days. Then, I will come in and stir things up and defeat my bitter foe, Dr. Patel."

They both laughed, and David said, "I am sure you can, but you are going to have to focus your attention here to do it. I know the two of you are friends, but we still need to get better ratings than WWN and you have to stay ahead of Raza."

Technically, President Willets had not directly asked Sybil to begin the interrogation of Adm. Jennings, but it fell within her purview.

The prisoner had been sitting in the darkened cell in Loudoun County, Virginia and refusing to speak to anyone except to repeat his mantra—"I demand to see a lawyer. I am a senior naval commander, and I demand a JAG officer and a navy hearing. I am an American citizen, and I know my rights,"—to anyone who even passed by his cell. No one spoke a word to him.

Sybil took her place behind the two-way mirror, and Mac Young brought the handcuffed and hooded prisoner into the room. Mac wore a Darth Vader Halloween mask. He secured the wrist cuffs to an "O" ring on the table top and the ankle shackles to an "O" ring bolted to the steel floor.

Sybil chose her Betty Boop voice from the options offered by her portable voice distortion machine and began to speak, "Prisoner US13-20/("slash") 20-Nev-Out. I am your interrogator for the first few years you spend here. Later you will be transferred to the most secure prison in the world. It is also the loneliest, and most boring one in the world."

"U.S.?" he asked, surprising Sybil that he would begin to speak so early in the interrogation.

"To be determined. We have a lot of questions, and you will give a lot of answers before we get to those sorts of decisions.

"I demand to see a lawyer. I am a senior naval commander— my name is Vice-Admiral Duncan Lloyd Jennings. I am the DCNO—Deputy Chief of Naval Operations—the N2/N6 and the DNI—director of naval intelligence—in the United States Navy—and I demand a senior JAG [Judge Advocate General] officer and a navy hearing. I am an American citizen, and I know my rights."

"I'm glad you brought all of that up. That gives me a chance to clear up some things for you. First, you are no longer anyone but Prisoner US13-20/("slash") 20-Nev-Out. You will never be anyone or anything else. You have no standing in any organization, no rank, no title, no responsibility. All of that is nothing I need to know about. People sitting where you are often lie, and I have no interest for the time being in your past—true or lie. Second, you may have once been an

American citizen. I neither know nor care about that—again, that could be from the past; but you may forget about it if it is true. Finally, you have no rights that I do not give you. It should be of passing interest to you to know that you are dead. Persons who need to know have your death certificate. I will share one thing from the past with you. Apparently, you were on some sort of ship, fell overboard and were lost at sea. A brief memorial was held for you. Try not to dwell on things you cannot change."

He started to repeat his mantra, "I am a senior..." and then the man in the Darth Vader helmet unlocked his wrist and ankle attachments from their "O" rings and shuffled him back to his cell where he remained hooded and shackled. The following day, and the day after were just as abrupt. He never got beyond the word, "senior." On the fourth day, he sat quietly.

Sybil's Betty Boop voice took up where she had left off three days ago, "Prisoner US13-20/("slash") 20-Nev-Out, I will now explain how the interviews will be conducted. I will ask a question, and you will answer. If you lie, you will lose two meals. Your trial has already been conducted; you were sentenced to life in prison without the possibility of parole; and the place of your confinement has been determined. Should you cooperate and tell us verifiable truth throughout, we will make some minor adjustments in the sentence. If you do not behave as you are told, you will remain here in these conditions until you do.

"First question, do you understand my instructions."

"Yes, but..."

"There are no buts. All answers are short and to the point without hedging."

"All right. Get on with it"

"Prisoner US13-20/("slash") 20-Nev-Out, did you run a heroin ring during your former employment?"

There was a long pause, but finally, a "no."

"Did you inveigle subordinates to commit crimes with you?"

"I am sure you know what I did."

"Say it."

"Yessss," he hissed

"Did you sell top secret United States information to al Qaeda operatives for money?"

That stopped Jennings. He was not sure until that moment that the navy knew about that."

There was another long painful pause, then a quiet, "yes."

"Did you cause the murders of five top-secret CIA agents during the past year?"

"Yes…but…"

"No buts. That will be all of the questions for today. Beginning bright and early tomorrow, "Prisoner US13-20/ ("slash") 20-Nev-Out, you will enter the room where you are now sitting and you will type out every detail of every crime and every treasonous act that you and your partners in crime committed. You are dismissed.

Back to the dark silent cell. Because he had answered that day's questions, he had three meals—if you could accurately call what was brought to him a "meal."

Sybil worked every morning at Wolf News and every afternoon at the site in Virginia. Other agents took the afternoon and evening shifts. Sybil worked herself out of a job in three months.

She received three serious offers during the fourth month after she first started the Jennings interrogations. First, Wolf News offered her a vice-presidency in charge of major topical and new series. Second, Columbia University College of

Medicine offered her a position as dean of the medical school and a full professorship. The DCIA offered her the DDCIA job when Andrew Dillon retired in December, 2015. The last and most tantalizing offer came from President Parker Conrad Willets.

"Would you consider succeeding Surgeon General, Milton Armstrong, Dr. Norcroft?"

These were all "take-it-or-leave-it" offers which, by their very nature, once chosen closed off other avenues of her career. There was no room for compromise. This was not a "life is a bowl of Munichs," as H.L. Mencken said, but more of the nature of Robert Frost's "Two roads diverged in a yellow wood, and sorry I could not travel both and be one traveler, long I stood and looked down one as far as I could to where it bent in the undergrowth; then took the other, as just as fair…"

"Ah, decisions," she sighed, decisions."

-The End-

Sybil Norcroft Book Five

Decisions

Sybil Norcroft, M.D., Ph.D., F.A.C.S., achieves one of her life's great ambitions; she is nominated and confirmed to become the surgeon general of the United States. As usual in Sybil's complicated life, things are not entirely as they seem. The president puts her in that prominent position to further her real career as a super-secret, super-spy. Her new position puts her in a nearly perfect position to get close to the elite of Saudi Arabia, including the movers and the shakers of their intelligence and defense systems. She enters into a world of subterfuge, lies, betrayal, and overt espionage that puts her in the line of fire.

Sybil learns that she is out of the pan and into the fire. The nation and the world descend into the throes of an H5N1 influenza pandemic that is the same strain that decimated the earth during WW I. The position of quarantine officer in chief devolved to Sybil Norcroft, M.D., Ph.D., F.A.C.S., Surgeon General of the United States, making her the most despised figure in the country. That unwelcome reputation is magnified exponentially when the president declares martial law. In the heat of the battle over that most highly unpopular presidential order, Sybil and the president are impeached and brought before the Senate to determine what will become of them. As she faces down disgrace, despair, and perhaps even prison, Sybil gets a stirring call to arms by her loyal husband.

"Sybil, you know this is a time of big decisions for you. I know that the president has asked you to be his next director of the CIA. What you have to decide is whether or not you can get off the porch and run with the big dogs."